FALCON BOOKS

Patty and Jo
The Case of the Toy Drummer
BY JANET KNOX

When Patty and Jo Faraday returned to Harker's Cove, the scene of their exciting adventure with an escaped convict, it was for a fun-filled summer vacation. It started gaily, with a birthday party at which the Faraday twins received a lovely music box with a toy drummer on top. But the toy drummer had a strange history, and one day he disappeared. How Patty and Jo caught a mysterious prowler and found out what the toy drummer really was makes gay and exciting reading.

Other FALCON BOOKS for Girls:

"The toy drummer is gone!"

Patty and Jo

The Case of
the Toy Drummer

by JANET KNOX

THE WORLD PUBLISHING COMPANY

Cleveland and New York

Falcon Books

are published by THE WORLD PUBLISHING COMPANY

2231 West 110th Street · Cleveland 2 · Ohio

Contents

The Case of the Toy Drummer

1 Return to Harker's Cove

How DIFFERENT the landscape looks now in early summer. Remember, Jo, how every single thing was completely covered with white snow when we made this trip the first time?" Patty turned her dark curly head away from the train window to regard her twin sitting on the opposite seat.

"Yes, now the bleak whiteness has given way to those cool, green fields and the deeper green of the woods. Oh, Welty, how soon will we be there?"

The Faraday twins both appealed to their guardian who grinned merrily at their eagerness. "Harker's Cove is the next stop, girls. That's only an hour's ride to go." Welton Duer was inwardly thanking his lucky stars for all the good fortune the past six months had brought him. For, he asked himself, what had he done to deserve his charming wife and two such lovely daughters? A short half-year ago I was a lonely, middle-aged bachelor holding only bitterness against the world, he thought to himself.

He looked across at Mavis whose head was bent over a book, unaware of his scrutiny. Her figure was like that of a girl, small and slim. As a matter of fact, she looked as if she might be the twins' older sister. Even to the color of her hair she resembled them, although hers was straight while Jo and Patty often mourned over the unruliness of their curly locks.

What a pity, Welton sighed to himself, that we didn't marry when we were both young. But no, I had to be stubborn, I had to be free in order to make long archeological expeditions which made a normal married life impossible. He pounded his fist softly against the arm of the seat.

Mavis looked up from her book with a questioning glance at her husband. "Did you just think of something we've forgotten, dear?"

"What?—N-no," he said, coming out of his reverie. "I was just telling myself what a fool I've been. You know, I see no reason why you can't come along with me on these research trips I have to make now and then. That is, if you would want to. And, of course, only when there was no danger involved. Oh, I don't mean right away, you understand." He hesitated, waiting to see how Mavis would react to such a suggestion.

"Why, I think it's a splendid idea. Winters when the girls are in school we'd both be at loose ends, not knowing what to do with ourselves."

"We might even take them along sometime," Welton went on eagerly. "Now that I think of it, your father used to take you everywhere with him, didn't he?" He turned to Pat at his side.

"You bet," she grinned. "Wherever his engineering was needed. In New Mexico, Texas, Panama, even South America once."

"We liked that best of all," Jo added, remembering those carefree days when school was secondary to the first-hand lessons of experience they had had. "It was perfectly grim when we first went to Miss Langton's school. And then later—" Jo preferred not to remember when their father had not returned. He had died of a fever contracted in Central America.

The twins' mother had died when they were born, but of course they had pictures of her, and their father had talked of her often. Since their father, a construction engineer, had to travel most of the time, he was forced to leave his daughters in the care of their great-aunt Harriett. She was a woman who recognized her duty, but she did not really love children. Her cold, forbidding house was never a home to them although Patty and Jo lived with her until they were eight years old. On one of his brief visits Mr. Faraday realized how unhappy his children were and he abruptly gathered their few belongings and took them wherever his work called him. Next followed two years of carefree, nomadic living that enabled the twins to be close to their father and, at the same time, gave them experience which taught them many things about people and places they would not have learned from books.

Then Mr. Faraday was assigned to a building project in the jungles of Central America and he regretfully decided it was no place to take two little girls. Instead he sent them to Miss Langton's school and promised to be back in a year. It was during this trip to Central America that tragedy struck and the twins found themselves alone, with only an unseen, mysterious guardian to look after their needs.

Vacation times became ordeals until, as related in *Patty and Jo, Detectives*, the sixteen-year-old Faraday twins were invited to spend their Christmas vacation at their guardian's lodge. Looking forward eagerly to a gay two weeks of fun, the girls found, on their arrival at the faraway Michigan village, that Welton Duer had left the previous day on business. Would they never set eyes on the man who governed their welfare? Firmly convinced that Duer's departure was strange, the twins purposefully set out to find the reasons for his disappearance.

Although the girls were alike in physical appearance, the similarity did not carry over completely into their characters. While Pat possessed an imaginative mind, Jo was clear-thinking and realistic. In this way, the personality of one complemented that of the other.

It was Pat's imagination which first set the twins on the trail of mystery. She was sure that the Japanese servant, Yamoto, and Mrs. Gruber, the housekeeper, knew more than they were willing to tell. After a series of exciting adventures involving even a skirmish with an escaped convict, the twins solved the mystery of Welton Duer's disappearance. Together with their newfound friend, Dick Prentiss, they were instrumental in reuniting their guardian with his former sweetheart, Mavis Martin. Mavis and Welton had included the twins in their future and offered the girls their home. All too soon it was time for Patty and Jo to return to school for the final semester, but they were happy in the knowledge that when graduation came in June they would have a real home to go to.

"Well, we'll have plenty of time to decide these things later," said Mavis. Then, looking at her watch, she said, "Better get your things together now, girls, we're nearly there."

Immediately there followed a flurry of con-

fusion while Patty and Jo retrieved scattered
magazines and miscellaneous belongings. Their
laughter filled the railroad car when their heads
bumped together during a scramble under the seat
for one of Jo's gloves. The rest of the passengers
smiled at their gaiety, for the twins unconsciously won friends everywhere by their warm-
heartedness and good humor. They finished
assembling their luggage just as the conductor
announced their stop.

Welton Duer alighted first. He carefully helped
Mavis down the steps, then Jo and Patty. Spying
a familiar old car parked next to the small station,
the girls raced over to greet Yamoto who stood
waiting and trying vainly to suppress a wide grin.

"Welcome home, Mliss Patty, Mliss Jo. Welcome, Mlisteh Dueh—and," he grinned even more
broadly, "Mliss Dueh." Yamoto made a deep bow
before them and Mavis colored a little.

"Gee, it's great to be back," sighed Jo, looking
about happily.

"Smell those pines, Jo," cried Patty enthusi-
astically. "Isn't it heavenly? Doesn't it provoke
memories?"

While the girls continued their babbling,

Welton Duer and Yamoto collected their baggage from the stationmaster and stowed it away in the rear of the car. In a few minutes they were ready to start the last lap of their journey home.

"Are you going to stand there all afternoon, or shall we be on our way?" Mavis laughingly interrupted the girls when she saw that Yamoto was anxious to leave.

"Oh, of course we're not, Mavis," Patty said, answering the first question, and she pushed Jo ahead of her into the back seat of the car. Mavis followed after them and Welton settled himself beside Yamoto.

"Not too crowded back there, are you?" Welton asked. "All the luggage wouldn't fit in the trunk so we had to put a couple of the bags on the floor there."

They all assured him everything was all right, so with a few rumbles and jerks the car responded to Yamoto's coaxing. Only Yamoto seemed to be able to handle the temperamental old car. Welton Duer had threatened time and again to sell it for junk, but at the mere suggestion of such a thing Yamoto looked pained. For, although his duties were primarily to keep the Lodge running smoothly, he prided himself on his knowledge of all things mechanical. And a good thing it was, too, since Welton's patience became sorely tried when the toaster didn't work or the clock was slow. Contrariwise, he could study a single fossil or ancient inscription for hours at a time without losing his zeal if he could not solve its problems.

Yamoto had also added supervision of Patty and Jo to his list of duties. He had quickly grown attached to them, liking their adventurous spirits. The twins had returned his friendship, aware of his loyalty to them. His watchful eye was always upon them, ready to protect or defend if necessary. Had the girls known this, however, it is possible they would have resented it slightly, since they loved to do things that might seem a bit dangerous in the eyes of others. Yamoto's silent ways were never without purpose they had soon learned.

A crisp breeze told the occupants of the car that they were nearing the lake and Harker's Cove. Then they were flying along the cliff road and presently the Lodge driveway made a gap in the trees on the left. They could see Mrs. Gruber on the porch looking a little less morose than was usual for her.

"Well, I'm glad to see you arrived safely," she greeted them. "Your train must have been a little late for I've been watching for you some time now. Come in, come in, I've had lunch all ready for you. I hope it hasn't been spoiled by being held back this way."

"I'm sure it will be fine, Mrs. Gruber," said Mavis soothingly. "We're all famished."

"She hasn't changed a bit," Jo whispered to Pat and giggled softly.

"Sh-h-h. She'll hear you," cautioned Pat.

"If you'll each take one of these bags into your room, we can eat right away," said Welton, as he came up behind them with his hands full of luggage. "Yamoto and I will manage the rest."

"Okay." Both girls seized their own suitcases and followed Welton into the house. In their room they saw that either Yamoto or Mrs. Gruber had thoughtfully placed a vase of fresh flowers on the chest of drawers. It was a cheerful room with the June sun streaming in the windows. They swiftly combed their hair, freshened themselves a little and joined Mavis and Welton for lunch.

The twins were surprised to find they were more than a little tired from their trip. They quickly accepted Mavis' suggestion of a nap after lunch.

"That will give me a chance to get some work done. My bones are waiting," Welton joked, in reference to his fossil collections.

"Then we'll leave you alone for an hour or so," his wife answered.

It was a pleasant feeling to sink down into comfortable beds once more, the twins thought. Although they had both completely enjoyed the journey home, as Pat remarked, "It's wonderful not to have to brace your feet against the lurches of those pullmans." Voices in the living room roused the girls from their nap later in the afternoon. They went out to find that Dick Prentiss and his mother were engrossed in conversation with Mavis and Welton. The Prentisses had just returned from a trip East by automobile and had been present at the twins' graduation.

"This is a surprise. We thought you wouldn't be back for another week," Jo greeted them.

"Hi, twins. We made better time than we expected to," Dick answered. He stood up, smiling warmly, to greet the girls. He was a tall, good-looking boy of about eighteen, who had been Welton Duer's fishing and hunting crony since he was a youngster.

"We came over first thing," Dick went on. "Had to give you a welcome typical of this fair community." He spread his arms out expansively.

"Dick couldn't wait to let you get settled," his mother said, turning to explain to Mavis who sat beside her in the couch. "I hope you'll excuse his overwhelming enthusiasm for your twins here. My stars, I never knew him to take such a liking to a pair of girls this way."

Dick grinned back a little sheepishly at his mother, but was quick to remark, "These kids aren't the usual sort, you know, Mom. Welty found that out, didn't you?"

And now it was Welton's turn to look embarrassed, for he had insisted that there was no place in his life for "women with a capital letter" as he phrased it. Instead of answering Dick's question, he said, "Why don't you young upstarts just take yourselves out of here? Isn't it the limit, Mrs. Prentiss, the way the younger generation shows no respect for its elders?" He glowered at the three, but the hint of laughter in his voice did not convince anyone that he meant what he had said.

"I know when I'm not appreciated," Dick retorted, assuming an air of injured pride. "If you brought your swim suits, girls, let's go down to the beach."

"Isn't it a little early in the season for swimming?" Mavis looked a little concerned. "Pat and Jo aren't used to the chilly waters of our lake, and that sun isn't making it as warm as it appears to be."

"I went in for a dip this morning to test it for you. Nope, it's fine if you don't stay in too long, and we won't."

"Well, then, run along and have a good time."

As the three left the Lodge chattering simultaneously, Mavis laughed and turned back to face Mrs. Prentiss. "Welty tries so hard to play the role of a disciplinarian, though I'm afraid he's no actor."

"You'll do well to take lessons in managing these young adults from Mavis, Welton. She speaks their language."

"But she's just like one of them, that's the

trouble," Welton grumbled. He put his arm around Mavis' shoulder to show he really didn't mind. "It only adds to the problem. I have three children instead of just two. I—I give up."

"Take my advice and let Mavis handle them," Mrs. Prentiss insisted. "Now, where were we?"

"The party," Welton reminded her. "All you want me to do is to devise some scheme to get Jo and Pat out of the way while you make the arrangements, right?"

"Yes, dear." Saying this, Mavis stood up and walked in the direction of the dining room. "That way they won't possibly suspect that we're planning a surprise for their birthday. And you know what suspicious natures they have!"

"How old did you say they were going to be?" Mrs. Prentiss asked.

"Seventeen. Now, since everything's settled, let me get you a cup of tea." Mavis turned and walked through the dining room to the kitchen where she found Mrs. Gruber had already set out the tea things.

Meanwhile Patty and Jo were sampling the offerings of the small lake resort. It was quite a long walk from the Lodge to the beach. The path led them down the side of the cliff in a winding course made necessary because of the almost sheer drop. Here and there small outcroppings of earth and rock leveled the path somewhat and provided space for the growth of scrub pines.

Dick led the way, showing little regard for the hazards of the tortuous trail. He seemed more or less to be leaving the girls to manage as best they could to keep up with his striding gait. About halfway down they overtook him on one of the level stretches.

"We're not so different from other girls that we're cousins to mountain goats," Jo said a little irritably. She stooped to rub a scraped place on her ankle.

"Gee, I'm sorry, Jo. I guess I just didn't realize how bad this path would seem to someone who's not used to it. It's as safe as can be, really. What's the matter with your leg?"

"Nothing's the matter with it," she snapped, "I skinned my ankle on your safe old trail." Jo was not going to be placated so easily.

"You were barreling along at quite a pace,

Dick," Patty admonished gently. "We're here for the summer—at least, we wanted to be. Now, I wonder if we'll last."

"Forgive me, both of you, for being so stupid." He really looked crestfallen, for he had planned on a summer of fun with the girls and here he was spoiling things already.

"My, what a honey of a lake!" exclaimed Jo, suddenly willing to forget her injured ankle and pride. Below the scrub pine a clear green lake shimmered in the bright sunlight. The water gently lapped at the rim of the shore. Clean white sand extended perhaps twenty feet back from the water, forming a kind of frame. It was, indeed, enough to make one forget a petty squabble.

"It's even nicer to swim in," Dick replied. "If you're rested now, we can go down and you'll see for yourselves."

This time Dick carefully took each girl by the hand and helped them over the bumpy stretches of the path. In a few minutes they reached the bottom of the cliff where Dick showed them the dressing shacks tucked underneath the cliff to one side. Since few of the summer visitors had yet arrived, the three young people had the beach to themselves.

Not much time passed before Patty and Jo emerged from one of the dressing rooms, clad in their swim suits. Jo's suit was turquoise blue while Pat's was coral, making an attractive combination.

"Humph, I thought twins always dressed alike," was Dick's only comment.

"That's old stuff," sniffed Patty. Then she laughed and Dick relented by giving her an approving whistle.

Seizing each girl by an arm, Dick pulled them giggling into the water. "If there's anything I can't stand, it's a girl who dilly-dallies around before getting into the water. I had to make sure you wouldn't."

Two white caps bobbed up out of the water to hear this outburst. "You needn't have worried," Pat said merrily. "We love to swim. How deep does it get?"

"Oh, it's about forty feet deep in some parts, but that's way out in the middle. Have no fears, though, there's a mighty competent lifeguard on duty all season. It so happens that that's me—mornings, anyway. You're quite safe."

"I'm not so sure about that," Jo answered him quickly, remembering the journey down the cliff.

"Is that a float I see out there?" Pat interrupted. "Come on, I'll race you for it!"

Dick sat swinging his legs from the platform as Pat pulled herself up, dripping, beside him. Jo finished a close third in the race, taking the loss with good grace. "I'm just a little rusty, I guess. You wait, Mr. Prentiss, until I regain my form and then I'll give you something to grin about."

"I don't doubt it for an instant, Miss Faraday."

"What are you two being so formal about? Jo's not kidding, though, usually she beats me."

"Say, your lips are getting a little blue, Pat. You've had enough for today. I promised Mavis that I'd only allow you a little swim."

"I guess it is colder than I thought. It's the wind that makes it that way. Golly," another thought suddenly struck her. "Mavis is a peach, isn't she?"

"Best there is," Dick said lightly as he dove expertly into the water. "Coming?"

"We're really a couple of lucky kids, do you

know that, Pat?" Jo, too, became suddenly serious. She stared down into the glistening water for another moment in silence. "To have one set of wonderful parents is something to be thankful for, but to have two sets—we must be leading charmed lives." With that she followed Dick into the water and swam slowly back to shore.

2 *Making New Friends*

You really ought to have another pair of warm slacks," Mavis remarked the following morning, as she helped the twins unpack their luggage. "My goodness, what is this?" she exclaimed, holding up a large ball of socks tied around the middle with string.

"That's our head," Jo explained. Seeing the puzzled look on Mavis' face, she said, "You know, the mummified one Welty gave us for Christmas last year. We didn't want it to be smashed."

"Now I remember. But you can't blame me for thinking it an odd way to pack socks. Where shall I put it?"

"I'll take it," Jo said, holding out her hand. "How I shuddered the first time I saw this on the little table in the living room! To think of some long-dead jungle headhunter prizing this as a sign that he had killed one of his enemies seemed horrible to me. Now I'm rather fond of it." As she talked Jo carefully untied the string and separated the socks. From this gaily colored nest the shriveled human head seemed to grin incongruously up at her. Smiling to herself she laid it on the top of the chest of drawers.

"It might not be a bad idea to wrap your own head in that fashion, Jo," Patty called from the closet where she was hanging up blouses. "Conserve what precious little brains you have."

"Funny thing that so few people can really tell us apart," Jo remarked to no one in particular. A snort from Pat told her, however, that the remark did not go unnoticed.

"Getting back to the slacks I mentioned, the mornings are cold up here, even in July. One pair apiece will hardly be enough." Mavis fingered the pair she was arranging on a hanger. "Pat, find me a piece of paper and a pencil, please, and we'll start making a list of things you need. Welty must have some in his den."

"These winter things I'll just pile here on the bed, Mavis. Oh, dear, I wish they hadn't delivered our trunks so promptly. Here is everything we own all to be stowed away somehow or other." Jo sighed and picked up another dress from the trunk before her while Pat went in search of paper and pencil.

Tapping gently on the door, Pat went into the study at Welton's sign of recognition. She knew he didn't like to be interrupted at work and intended to make her mission as brief as possible. Welton, his wide brow furrowed in concentration, was bending over a large walnut desk.

"Sit down, child, sit down. I'll be finished here in just a moment," he said, without raising his eyes.

Patty glanced around the room quickly. Following his orders in this particular case was not easy. To anyone who did not know Duer's habits it would have seemed impossible for him to think among the confusion that surrounded him. The desk itself was littered with scraps of paper, some of them crumpled, and with boxes of rock speci- mens, reference books and several stub-ends of pencils. The rest of the room was equally clut- tered. In front of the windows stood a chest, equipped with special drawers to hold the sam- ples of his collection. Some of the drawers were pulled far out and left sagging precariously to- ward the floor; others were pushed in beyond the face of the chest. One whole wall was lined with bookshelves—the only orderly section in the study.

Yet, were you to ask Welton how he managed to accomplish any work in the room he would have insisted that he could put his hands on any- thing he wanted and heaven help the person who disturbed his mess! Mindful of this, Patty gingerly lifted a sheaf of papers from the only remaining chair and held them in her hand as she waited, making a mental note to replace them when she left.

At last Welton looked up from the object in his hand. "What would you think of this, my dear?" He held out toward her what looked to be an ordinary slab of stone.

"Why, I don't know, it looks like just an old rock to me," she answered. "That's not a very scientific answer, I admit."

"I quite agree."

"I'm sorry, but we didn't learn too much about your branch of science in school, Welty. Mostly chemistry and biology, you know."

"To be a daughter of mine, you'll have to do better than that." Patty smiled happily at the relationship he had implied. "Now," Welton cleared his throat and assumed the voice of a platform lecturer, "this is a specimen of petrified wood. You know what that is, don't you?"

"No, sir," came the answer in a small voice matching that of a timid schoolgirl.

"Petrified wood is wood that—I—well—that is petrified, of course. Everyone knows that."

"Do you mean wood from a tree that has had the small particles of cellulose replaced by grains of minerals until gradually, over a period of thousands of years, the tree has turned to stone?

A hearty laugh reverberated in the room and reached even Mavis and Jo in the bedroom beyond. "Well, well, the joke's on me this time."

Welton pulled out his handkerchief to wipe the tears from his cheeks.

"To be honest with you, Welty, it only just happened that I found one of your books fallen behind the radio last night and after I had fished it out I started to leaf through it. Then I got so interested that I read quite a lot of it after I went to bed. You can ask Jo about that, because she was mad at me for leaving the light on so long."

"Hmmm, so you found the subject interesting, eh? Well, we'll see about that. Now, to what do I attribute the honor of this visit? In short," he added pompously, "what did you want?"

"Oh," Pat answered hastily, "Mavis needs some paper and a pencil. She said you'd have some we might use."

"Of course, here you are." And, confidently opening the top drawer of the desk, he felt around for the desired articles. He took his hand out again after pushing a few things around and looked bewildered. Then his eyes roved the desk top. "Ah." He picked up one of the pencil stubs and reached under the tallest stack of papers for a torn piece of an old manila envelope. "Will these do?"

"Okay for a shopping list, I guess. Thanks." Pat blew him a kiss as she retreated to the doorway. "Oh, gee, I almost forgot. Here." She returned and laid the papers she was holding in her hand back on the chair.

"Ten minutes to find these?" Jo asked Pat, wrinkling her nose at what she considered shameful tardiness.

"We got to talking about something else," Pat retorted vaguely.

"This will be fine," Mavis laughed. "I know what happened. Welty got off on his favorite subject. Maybe I had better head this list with a set of scratch pads for myself!"

"Sometimes I wonder how he got along so long without us, don't you?"

"Stop thinking so hard and help me with this load of *your* sweaters," Jo chided her.

Pat fell to work with a will and soon order was again restored. Mavis finished her list and was rechecking it when Welton looked in from the hallway.

"Anyone here interested in a little tramp

through the woods? Can't seem to settle down to work today. Nothing clears the mind like a good walk in fresh air."

"That's for me," Jo said, groaning a little as she straightened up. "All morning that glorious sunshine has been fairly begging for a sympathetic soul like mine to take advantage of it."

"Maybe we could help you, Welty." This came from Pat. "That is, if you'd let us. Wouldn't we, Jo?"

"Gee whiz, sure. The only trouble is we don't know one fossil from another. At least, I don't. Here, catch." She picked up a sweater for herself from the bed and tossed another one over to Pat.

The two girls just stood for a moment on the top porch step when they first went outside. The garden was ablaze with color, intensified by the bright sunlight, but a cool wind blew across the lake and they were glad they had remembered to wear sweaters. The breeze gently pushed the branches at the tops of the tall trees overhead, as the party of four walked along through the woods. It was the same trail that the Faradays had followed six months before, although then it had looked quite different. Had it not been for the hunting shack which they both recognized as Welton's "hideout" the girls would have found it difficult to believe. Squirrels and many varieties of birds put forth a noisy chatter high over their heads. At the level of their feet they could detect the scurrying sounds of what were undoubtedly rabbits and other small game.

Presently the group came to the banks of a small river and stopped. "Since you've expressed such an interest in my work, we might just as well have our first lesson in geology this morning. Right here beside this river is a good place to begin."

"Why, Welty?" asked Pat, coming closer to the edge of the river bank. "I don't see any interesting-looking rocks here."

"Perhaps you don't, Patty, but do you know what an important part rivers play in the formation of rocks?"

She and Jo both shook their heads.

"Millions of years ago when the earth was formed, it was hot. Gradually it cooled and shrank and in this cooling process the earth buckled in some places to form our great mountain systems. Next came the formation of water—

seas, lakes and streams. These small streams at first just ran along the top of the earth until they managed to carve out beds to flow in. Next they widened the beds, taking earth from the sides and depositing it on the bottom or perhaps even carrying some of it all the way to the sea. Layers and layers of small grains of earth, or sediment, gradually came to be deposited in this way. And do you know what happened then?"

"You did say this had something to do with the formation of rocks," Jo said slowly, "but I'm not sure I see the connection yet."

"Yes, it does have a great deal to do with rock formations. You see, after the winter snows melted, sometimes these streams we are talking about became swollen and overflowed their banks. When that happened the stream often did not go back into its old course, but, instead, it carved out a new bed. As a result the banks of the old stream were covered with earth and the sediment was pressed down hard. Years and years later rocks had been formed. That is how sandstone and limestone and shale are made. We classify them all as sedimentary rocks."

"I see, sedimentary because they are made

from sediment. Is that it?" Pat's face wore an intent look.

"Is this same process taking place right now?"

"It is. Although it will take millions of years and just the right sort of conditions for the sediment deposited by this river to become rock."

"What about other kinds of stone—like granite and marble, for instance? Are they formed in the same way?" Jo questioned him.

"No, those are formed beneath the earth's surface. Have you girls ever seen a volcano?"

"Sure, once in Mexico Dad took us way up to the top of one where we could look down inside it. I remember how scared I was, looking way, way down deep into the very middle of it." Jo hesitated a moment in concentration. Then she said slowly, "Oh, I see, when a volcano erupts, you mean, that stuff, what do you call it, lava, I think, comes out and . . ."

"Exactly. Then the air cools and solidifies it into rock. And that is what we geologists believe happened when the earth cooled after it was first formed. Great masses of molten material on and near the surface cooled and hardened. Probably, there were many volcanoes which continued to erupt for a long time afterward. Rocks formed in this way are classified as igneous rocks. The word 'igneous' comes from the Latin word for fire."

"How clear it all becomes when you explain it, Welty," said Pat. "Much clearer than it was in the book I was reading last night. Now we know that rocks are formed by layers of sediment and by fire."

"There are variations, too, Pat. But I think we've gone far enough in our lesson for one day. We'd better be getting back home for lunch. Something tells me it's time. This afternoon, if you like, we'll look at some rock specimens I have in the study."

"Don't overload their minds, Welton," laughed Mavis. "Or you'll frighten them off."

"Nonsense, they're eager to learn about these things, as they should be," was his earnest reply.

During lunch while Yamoto was serving them, he remarked, "We need food flom village, Mliss Glubeh said. Shall I dlive in today, Mliss Dueh?"

"Please do, Yamoto," Mavis answered. "And why don't you take Pat and Jo with you? They haven't seen much of the village—not that there is much to see."

"Yes, Mliss. Be leady two o'clock please, Mlissy Patty and Jo?"

"But we were going to look at Welty's rocks, Mavis," Pat protested.

"There will be plenty of afternoons for that, my dears," Welton interrupted, after receiving a look from Mavis that meant "let me have my way."

"Tell Mrs. Gruber I'll help her with the list after lunch, Yamoto, and the girls will be ready to go when you are."

Yamoto nodded and retreated to the kitchen. Later, true to his word, he gaily tooted the horn outside the front door of the Lodge at exactly two o'clock. Jo had been watching for him from the living-room window and now called to her sister.

"The sound ot that horn tells me Yamoto is getting impatient. Hurry *up*, Patsy!"

"I'm coming. I can't find my red jacket. Seen it, Jo?"

Jo giggled. "I sure have. I'm wearing it." By

mutual agreement they often wore each other's things, but it was usual to ask for them first. "You can wear my red cardigan if you must have something red," Jo suggested.

"Okay, I'm ready." Pat emerged from the bedroom wearing the sweater over a crisp white blouse and flared gray cotton skirt. The automobile horn tooted once again, this time even more insistently.

"We can all sit in front, can't we?" Jo asked, as she plopped down next to Yamoto.

"Yes, Mlissy." He grinned at his two charges as he reached across them to pull the door closed. Then he put the car in gear and they were on their way.

The drive to the village was a short one and the road they followed was lined on either side with giant shade trees. At intervals these trees arched and met in the middle, reminding Patty of an aisle in a cathedral.

While Yamoto attended to the groceries, he suggested that the girls walk around and do a little exploring. When this was settled they agreed to meet him at the car in an hour or so.

"Let me see, now, which way shall we go, Jo? Toward that sign that says 'Telegraph Office' or toward the one lettered 'Gifts'?"

"Does it really matter too much?" Jo laughed. "Since this is the village square, we'll pass them both in either case. But I think I can guess what's in the telegraph office. Let's walk the other way. Gifts sound more interesting."

Off they went arm in arm. They walked slowly past the small stores, stopping now and then to window-shop. Even the window of the hardware store beckoned to them.

"It's strange when you stop to think of it, Jo. I mean, in a large city who would bother looking at tools and things unless, of course, you were going to buy something like that? Yet, here we are with our noses pressed against the glass deciding which garden trowel is the best buy."

"You're right, sis. I think it's because life goes on at a more leisurely tempo in towns like this. In bigger places everyone feels he has to rush hither and thither even if he's just going for a walk around the block."

"My, my, who would have expected to hear

such philosophizing here in Harker's Cove?"
came a voice from behind them.

The twins whirled to see who had been eaves-
dropping on their conversation. Prepared to be
annoyed by the intrusion, they came face to face
with Dick and two strangers.

"These are the Faraday twins, Pat and Jo, that
I was just telling you about, Elaine. Girls, this is
Elaine Anderson and her brother, George. They're
regular summer residents here."

Pat was sure right off that they were going to
like these two. A graceful girl about their age,
Elaine was a blue-eyed blonde with delicately
carved, perfect features. She looked almost arti-
ficial, but the way her mouth curved crookedly
when she smiled revealed that she was not merely
pretty to look at. She was mischievous, too. Her
brother was two years older, also blond, and had
a rather sober appearance at first glance. Closer
inspection, however, found that a pair of merry,
brown eyes and a sprinkling of light freckles
across the bridge of his nose belied his straight
lips and square chin. It was evident, also, that he
enjoyed the outdoors, for his face and arms were
already bronzed from the sun and weather.

When they had exchanged greetings, Dick announced, "It seems as if lunch time was hours ago. What do you say we all have a soda?" Seeing they were in agreement with his suggestion, he led the way into a small, clean-looking drugstore at the corner of the square. They each climbed up on a high stool at the counter and gave their orders to a pleasant boy on duty.

When their refreshments came, George first took a long sip of his malted, then asked, "Dick seems to know a good deal about you two, yet it's strange we never met before. In a place as small as this you're usually bound to know everybody in ten minutes and we've been here nearly a week."

Jo supplied the answer, explaining how she and Pat had been there only once before and then it was wintertime. "And we only just returned from school yesterday," she finished.

"I see," said Elaine. "No wonder we didn't know you then. We're only able to come here summers, although I've begged and begged Mother and Dad to come at Christmastime. But I thought Mr. Duer was a kind of an old recluse.

Dick insists not, though you know what a tease he is. Like that wild tale of yours," she stared accusingly at Dick, "that these girls had trapped a bandit!"

"That's the honest truth, I swear it." Dick raised his right hand above his head.

"Yes, really, it is true, not wild at all," Pat affirmed. She then told how they had stumbled across an escaped convict in the woods when they were actually looking for their guardian. Because it fitted Dick's version exactly, Elaine was ready to give in.

"Jeepers!" George exclaimed. "Let's hope you don't, as a rule, attract that sort of adventure."

"Look out for the Faradays, George," replied Dick, "if you don't like excitement."

"Say, Jo, there will be plenty of excitement if we don't hurry back." Pat looked aghast at the clock on the wall above. "Yamoto will be wondering what has become of us. Now, how could that hour fly by so quickly?" She shook her head as she picked up her purse.

"It's been so nice meeting you," Jo said as she warmly grasped Elaine's and George's hands.

"Yes, why don't you stop by our house tomorrow afternoon and we'll all go for a swim?" put in Pat.

They promised quickly to do so and the twins went flying down the street in the direction of the car.

3 Forgotten?

DURING THE following week, Patty and Jo found
that their days had begun to assume a rather
definite pattern. Mornings, they generally helped
Welton in his study by typing notes for him or
looking up things in his many reference books.
Pat slyly managed to make the room a little more
orderly without Welton becoming aware of the
change. Not a great deal of work was accom-
plished in these morning sessions, however, because the girls constantly asked endless questions.

The pleasure he derived from their inquisitiveness and interest more than made up for this as far as Welton was concerned. It stimulated him immeasurably. In turn, the girls appreciated his patient answers, although the full realization of how much they were learning undoubtedly was not apparent to them.

Their afternoon program generally included a swim with Dick Prentiss or the Andersons or just by themselves. The whole forest surrounding them had to be explored, too. Mavis joined them in many of their exploring trips and pointed out many interesting things they might otherwise have missed. She knew the region well and had an anecdote, a bit of history or a piece of gossip to relate about many parts of it.

The girls also discovered that Mavis was a well-traveled woman, having spent some time in Europe as a member of the Red Cross just after the war, and she had traveled extensively in the United States.

On the night that marked the end of their first week at the Lodge, Pat gloomily stared at her reflection in the mirror, her brush poised above her head, forgotten. Buttoning the top button of her pajamas and humming to herself, Jo stopped and looked up when she heard Pat heave a long sigh.

"Why such a sad face, twin?" she asked gently. She disliked seeing Pat unhappy and couldn't guess why she was at the moment.

"You mean you haven't been aware of what is happening? or, rather, hasn't happened?" Pat turned away from the mirror and faced Jo squarely.

"No," she answered bluntly. She frowned in concentration. "Nope, can't think of anything that hasn't happened that should. Tell me."

"You are insensitive, aren't you? Oh, me, I just wish I could be. Jo, don't you remember what tomorrow is? And they haven't said a word about it."

"Tomorrow?" Jo screwed up her face even more. Thinking out loud, she said, "Tomorrow is a week since we've been here, the date is the twentieth of June, what's so special about—June twentieth! Holy cow, it's our birthday!"

"Now don't you feel as utterly despondent as I do?"

"But, Pat, be sensible. How would Mavis and

Welty, the darlings, know that there was anything special about tomorrow? We didn't tell them."

"I am being sensible, I tell you." Her voice was shaking with emotion and she hated it. Whenever she was upset, her voice shook and that annoyed her even more. "I do try so hard to be less emotional and more like Jo," she thought to herself. Even knowing this, she resented being told to be sensible by the sensible member of the pair. Trying to compose herself, she said more softly, "Welty asked me even before we left Miss Langton's how old we were and I told him, 'Sixteen, nearly seventeen.' 'What do you call nearly seventeen?' he asked me and I told him when our birthday was."

"Oh," Jo said, catching a little of her sister's gloominess. She brightened up again immediately, however. "Listen here, Patty darling, we'll just have to pretend that tomorrow isn't any special day to us. Welty probably didn't remember what you said ten minutes after you said it. You know how absent-minded he is at times. You can't expect him to become a perfect substitute for our own dad overnight. It'll take time to train him." She laughed at her own feeble joke in an attempt to cheer up her sister. "Welty's taking us to a real country market town tomorrow, remember? When he planned this, you were as excited as anything, so let's just pretend that's our birthday present," she finally concluded. She yawned then and, seeing Pat was paying no attention to her, she shrugged her shoulders and climbed into bed.

At last Pat answered her in a dull voice. "I suppose that is the only thing we can do, but . . ." Her voice trailed away as she turned off the light switch. She lay there in the dark a long time, telling herself she was just being silly and Jo was right about such things. Jo's gentle, regular breathing in the bed beside her at last lulled her to sleep.

She was still a trifle solemn the following morning and Jo decided the best thing was to leave her alone. She had often found that Pat was likely to "snap out of it" by herself. Basically, Pat did not wish to be disagreeable and when she was, she knew it was unpleasant for her companions.

At breakfast Welton reminded Mavis that he was taking Patty and Jo away for the day. She seemed preoccupied that morning and for good reason, although the twins were not aware of it.

"Why don't you take a lunch along with you? Then you won't have to worry about finding a decent restaurant at noon. And if you see any nice early peas, you might pick out a few pecks for freezing."

"Do you want us to buy anything else? These farmers' products are as fresh as any you'll find any place. Meat? Eggs?"

"Eggs, yes. And anything else you want."

"That's a good suggestion for lunch," Welton replied. "Pat, honey, run out and ask Mrs. Gruber to pack us up a few sandwiches and some fruit. Tell her to fix whatever you think you'll like."

Pat nodded and excused herself from the breakfast table. Jo had already gone out to the garden for flowers she had promised to pick for Mavis.

When they were alone, Mavis frowned and said, "Pat seems troubled this morning. Jo, too. Do you think perhaps we were wrong to plan this little party as a surprise?"

"Troubled, you say? They didn't seem troubled

to me. You're only imagining things. Don't worry, everything is going to come off in fine style. I can feel it. Now, you're sure you can handle everything that needs to be done today?"

"Yes, Dick promised to come whenever I telephoned him. He arranged to switch his hours on duty at the beach, but didn't want to come until he was sure you'd be gone. Didn't want the girls to suspect anything. He'll help Yamoto move the furniture in the living room so that there will be room for dancing. Mrs. Prentiss is making the favors and I'm going to make the cake. Mrs. Gruber says she can handle the rest of the food, but just as sure as she tries to bake a cake, special, it will fall."

Welton chuckled at this. "Disaster is that woman's middle name. Well, I'll go collect my charges, then, and we'll soon be out of the way, if you're sure you're all set."

"Yes, the sooner you can get away the sooner we can begin. You know, I had an awful time yesterday, explaining to them why the house was being cleaned so thoroughly at the beginning of the week. They know that Yamoto has such an unswerving routine that it was an unusual occurrence. Thanks to Yamoto, I got out of it." She picked up her coffee cup and drained it. "He said their friends came in and out of the house so much and tracked in such quantities of sand that he had to clean twice as often. He pretended to be angry and I guess it was convincing. At least they kept out of his way afterward."

"Intrigue and undercover stuff," Welton snorted. "It is a wonder those two haven't caught on to our plan. Their detective instinct must be deteriorating."

Jo scraped her shoes carefully before she came into the house with her arms full of flowers. The garden was just beginning to show signs of promise and she had had to confine herself mainly to roses. The annual flowers, of course, had not yet started to blossom. Jo shook some of the dew from the petals, then pulled open the screen door trying not to lose any of her load.

"Aren't these gorgeous? Look at this big yellow one. Isn't it perfect? Here, Welty, take a whiff. Careful, don't prick yourself." She held out the bouquet to him.

He leaned over and inhaled deeply. " 'A rose is

a rose.' Gertrude Stein was right. There is no other flower quite like it."

"Who?"

"Gertrude Stein? She was a writer who did what many people thought were strange things with language. She was before your time, I'm afraid. Are you almost ready to go? Where's Patty?"

"I don't know, but I'll look. Patty!" she called as she went toward the kitchen with her flowers. "Pat? Where are you? Oh! Look out!"

Just as Jo approached the swinging door separating the kitchen from the dining room Pat pushed from her side, barely missing Jo's nose. "Oops! Sorry, I didn't hear you soon enough to stop."

Pat passed her sister and opened a drawer of the sideboard. She took out a tablecloth and went back into the kitchen where Mrs. Gruber was finishing the lunch.

"Where can I put these, Mrs. Gruber?" asked Jo, waving the flowers.

"Right there on the table will be fine. I'll put them in water just as soon as I finish wrapping these sandwiches. You know that little woven basket that hangs in the cellarway? Will you get it for me?"

"Sure thing."

"How does this sound to you, Jo?" her sister called after her. "Ham and cheese, peanut butter and jelly, hardboiled eggs, cookies, oranges and lemonade."

"Scrumptious." Jo came back with the basket which she handed to Mrs. Gruber. "Welty's ready to go. You ready?"

"Yes, as soon as I tuck this tablecloth around the top. There." She patted the gay blue-and-white plaid cloth on top and slipped her arm through the handle of the basket. Jo noticed that she seemed to be over her "pout" and was glad. She hated to see the day spoiled.

"Let me take that basket, Pat," offered Welton when the two reappeared from the kitchen. "Ooh," he groaned, "this feels like a sizable lunch."

"Gee, isn't Yamoto coming today?" Jo asked, for she saw they were not taking the rattletrap that was Yamoto's special charge. Parked at the bottom of the step was Welton's station wagon that he used on his archeological expeditions.

"Not this time he isn't. I thought I might have my kids all to myself today."

With loud goodbys and much waving of hands, almost as if this were a real trip, the party rolled out of the driveway. The day was warm and sunshiny with only a few harmless, fleecy clouds floating in the sky. Once out on the open highway the smell of sweet clover mingled with the now-familiar scent of pines. They drove along for quite a while before anyone spoke. Patty and Jo always found so much to look at when they traveled that they preferred to watch first and talk about it later.

They had been driving for perhaps an hour through rolling farm lands when Pat broke the silence. "What did you say was the name of the town we're going to, Welty?"

"Lampson. It's the county seat and is centrally located so that the farmers all over this area have no great distance to travel with their produce. The town is small, but you'll find it's a busy place."

"Do they sell their stuff right out in the open?" Jo shouted her question from her place next to the open window where the wind created by the motion of the car partially deafened her. Pat, next to her, put her hands over her ears in mock despair.

"The farmers use a great open space near the center of Lampson. There they set up their stalls and, as you'll see, there is no set pattern of arrangement."

"It's not like a supermarket, you mean?" Pat giggled.

"Hardly. The reason, of course, is that the farmer who comes earliest secures the best spot for his stall." Welton slowed down to let a huge transport truck pass them.

Rounding the next curve, they saw the outskirts of a town and a sign WELCOME TO LAMPSON flashed by them on the right. Scattered houses dotted the surrounding landscape and abruptly they found themselves on the main street. Half-ton trucks, jeeps and even a few horse-drawn wagons were crowded along both sides of the narrow street. Welton had to drive carefully to squeeze through the small passageway remaining in the middle.

"I should have parked back a ways, we'll never

find a place along here." Welton scanned the street ahead. "Well, in that case, we'll turn into one of these side streets."

At the next corner they turned right and found ample space for the car. The walk down to the market space was long but pleasant. The girls felt in a holiday mood, but, moreover, there was an air of expectancy about the town itself. The people they passed were chatting gaily to one another, shouting greetings to friends on the opposite side of the street. Being naturally friendly, the two girls were frankly interested in the people they saw. Since they had often been alone during their childhood, they sought company even among strangers. They had once devised a game, years before, of imagining what a stranger was really like by the way he dressed or how he walked. Of course, they rarely had the opportunity of testing their accuracy in this game, but it kept them from thinking too much about their loneliness. By this time, the game had become a habit, so that they automatically made guesses concerning the passersby in this fascinating town.

"There goes a grain man. See him there, Patsy? That tall one."

"Pooh. That's a wild guess, sis. How can you tell one farmer from another?"

"Easy. Didn't you notice that he was chewing on a soda straw?"

"You! Oh, but look ahead, Jo," Pat whispered. A figure was coming toward them and now was only a few steps away. "There's a difficult one for you. Doesn't look like a farmer to me, or even a farmer's son."

"Right you are," Jo breathed, after the figure had passed them. "He's going in the wrong direction for one thing. And he looked so serious—everyone else seems happy. By the cut of his coat, I'd say he was European. Handsome, too, Pat, just right for you."

"Silly. Too thin for my taste, anyhow." Still, for some reason, the glimpse of the tall, slim, strange-looking youth aroused Pat's curiosity. She could not have explained why, out of all the people passing to and fro, she wished to know more about this one boy. The deep furrows in his brow which indicated intense concentration coupled with the frantic look in his eyes as he brushed past her set Pat to wondering. As Jo had remarked, his rough wool suit was of European cut and Pat thought now it was much too heavy for such a warm summer day. "Maybe he's a spy or something!" she said aloud suddenly to her sister.

"Who? Oh, are you still thinking of the dark-haired fellow we passed?" Jo asked, having dismissed the stranger more quickly than her twin. She caught Pat's mood and quickly agreed. "Possibly. He certainly looked mysterious."

They did not have time to discuss the possibility further, for at that moment Welton jostled Jo's elbow.

"Watch your step here, girls," Welton warned as they approached a busy cross street just preceding the square. "It's getting pretty crowded now and it's hard to judge where the curb ends. Let me take you both by the arm."

He steered them safely over to the other side of the street, and there they found themselves surrounded by carts and stalls of every size and description. Carrots, onions, celery, radishes and fresh garden lettuce were proudly displayed right next to several crates of live chickens and ducks. Several burlap bags of potatoes leaned crazily against some sacks of poultry feed. Small boys darted to and fro among the laden shoppers, making every step a hazardous venture. Some stall-keepers zealously kept up a continuous shout in praise of their wares, while others— timid ones, perhaps—stood silently waiting for customers.

Patty was excited by all the noise and the wonderful mixture of odors that assailed her nostrils. As she passed from one stall to another, the acrid smell coming from the direction of the poultry crates blended into the fresh, earthy fragrance of vegetables and was topped by the sickening perfume of quantities of sweet pea blossoms. The combination was truly intoxicating. For a few moments she gasped, longing for fresh, uncontaminated air. The stifling sensation wore off gradually as she became accustomed to it, although the sense of exhilaration remained.

Suddenly she looked around for Jo and found she was not beside her as she had believed. Frantically she searched the crowd beyond for Welton and her sister. How long, she thought, have I been standing here alone? She held her breath, then released it as she caught sight of Welton at last—only as far away as the next booth. And Jo was with him.

"No, that will be all, thanks. Oh, say, may I pick them up on my way out?" Pat heard Welton say as she rejoined the others, her face flushed.

Jo saw her first and exclaimed, "What's the matter, Pat? You look so funny."

"N-nothing, really. I-I just thought I'd lost you and got panicky, that's all." She mopped her damp forehead with her handkerchief and felt better.

"Let's hold on to each other's hands, Patsy. Gosh, I'd hate to lose you!"

"What's all this?" Welton asked as he heard Jo's last sentence. When they had told him, he shook his head and said solemnly, "It's all my fault. There I go getting absent-minded again. Yes, it would be a good idea to keep track of one another in this crowd. Now, this gentleman I was talking to when I should have been thinking about you tells me there is a livestock exhibition going on at the other end of the square. How would you like to see that?"

"Are there any horses?" Jo asked. "I do adore horses."

"Well, I don't know, though I hardly think so. We can go and see, however. This way."

Welton piloted the girls before him once more. While they walked pyramid fashion, he continued his conversation, awkward as it sometimes became.

"It's quite unusual, my dears, for a show of this kind to be held at this time of year. And they are mainly in connection with the annual county fair —excuse me, sir—that's in August. Perhaps we'll come then, too. There are prizes and—I'm awfully sorry—blue ribbons and that sort of thing—be careful of that barrel there, Jo—ah, this must be the place. Whew, I'm winded."

Jo and Pat doubled over with mirth. "Oh, Welty, how funny and dear you are!" Jo hugged him in apology for their amusement at his expense.

"W-what? What have I done now, you vixen!" Welton looked genuinely puzzled.

Pat regained her composure first and explained. "There you were, striding along and pushing us along in front, too, and shouting and puffing and begging people's pardons. Oh! Oh!" Her description sent her into renewed gales of laughter and Welton chuckled heartily, too.

"I'm just an old fool. Forgive me, darlings."

"Oh no you're not! Besides, we couldn't love you nearly so much if you were any different." Jo spoke earnestly.

He patted them both and gave them an affectionate squeeze. Then, pointing beyond, he said, "Why, I declare, Jo, you're in luck! There are some horses. No, not there, over further by the far fence. They may only be draft horses, will you mind?"

"Jeepers, no! I just love to look at them. They —they're so noble-looking, somehow."

They walked across a stretch of green grass and approached the enclosure where the horses were tethered. Sure enough, they were sturdy work horses for sale, and a group of men in faded overalls were clustered about the fence. A young boy within the area was kept busy leading one horse after another up to the fence so that the buyers could scrutinize them closely. From time to time, he slowly turned a horse in a small circle while the men murmured together in low tones.

Patty and Jo listened and watched. They heard one man say to his companion, "That one there's been mistreated badly. Look at his mouth. Torn to shreds it is."

"Some fellers don't know how to handle 'em, that's sure. Now, Jake, take a look at this one. There's a beauty. Not too old and hardly a bend to his back. Good strong legs, too. Hey there, boy!"

The youth came toward them, the horse walking stolidly behind him. When the boy stopped near the fence the horse immediately dropped his head to crop the grass. The girls could not hear the conversation between the men and the boy, but they guessed they wished to know the price being asked, or, perhaps, they were bargaining for a lower price.

Pat's interest soon waned, for she did not share Jo's intense admiration for horses. She was a skilled rider, but these heavy, awkward animals were far different from the mounts to which she was used. Once her thoughts began to wander, she realized how hungry she was.

"Heavens, Jo, haven't you seen enough? I'm

absolutely starved. Welty, can't you make her come away? She's positively hypnotized!"

"Yes, yes, Jo—my dear Jo, let us be on our way. It's long past lunch time." Welton plucked at her sleeve.

"W-what. Oh, gee! Do we have to go now." Seeing Pat's petulant countenance she relented. "Okay. Did someone say lunch? Lead me to it."

4 Surprises

MEANWHILE, back at the lodge there was great activity. As soon as the girls had left with Welton, Mavis had flown to the telephone. Dick Prentiss answered at the first ring. He was all ready, he said, and would be over in a few minutes.

True to his word, he arrived almost before Mavis had replaced the receiver on the hook. "Mother let me have the car," he explained, flinging off his jacket onto a nearby chair. "Don't tell her how fast I drove. She'd be furious."

"You should be careful, Dick," Mavis cautioned.

"Oh, I really wasn't driving very fast. Golly, you ought to see how some of the fellows at school tear around the campus. They're always getting tickets for speeding. Could be," he grinned, "that I don't because I haven't got a car there. I remember once last year the police nearly had a fit when they caught a couple of the boys racing one another right in town. I agree with you that that sort of thing is a little risky."

"Risky! That's a mild term for it. But come, I have work for us to do. The twins will be back before we've even started if we stand here talking all day."

Yamoto, Dick, Mavis and Mrs. Gruber made quick work of transforming the lodge in readiness for the party. The furniture in the large living room was pushed back into the corners of the room and the rug was taken up for dancing. The remaining furniture was moved into Duer's study. Dick made festoons of yellow and white crepe paper to string across the ceiling.

In the kitchen, Mavis prepared the birthday cake and when it came out of the oven, lightly browned, she decorated it with yellow and white icing to carry out the color scheme. On top of the cake she wrote: "Seventeen Birthday Wishes Each For Patty And Jo" and put on thirty-four candles ready to be lit at the proper time.

Mrs. Gruber set the table buffet style for the supper to be served and prepared what dishes she could ahead of time. In the afternoon, Dick went home to call for his mother and to change his clothes. Mavis rested a short while then and was looking refreshed when Dick returned with Mrs. Prentiss, the first of the guests to arrive.

Hardly had the last guest arrived when Welton drove into the driveway. The words "Surprise! Surprise!" greeted the astonished girls as they stepped into the transformed living room. They were speechless with pleasure.

Pat turned to Mavis, who was nearest her, and hugged her wordlessly.

Jo found her voice at last and said, "So that's why you pretended to be so mean yesterday, Yamoto, while you were cleaning."

Everyone roared. Yamoto's eyes twinkled with merriment; he was pleased with the success of his joke.

Jo took a step toward him and said with pretended fierceness, "And I had nearly made up my mind not to speak to you again."

During the ensuing general laughter, Patty and Jo noted the people in the room. The guests included all of their friends, some new, some old. Dick and Mrs. Prentiss were there, of course, and Tommy Hastings, whom they hadn't seen since they returned to Harker's Cove, and Elaine and George Anderson.

A mountain of gifts was waiting for them piled on the coffee table. "Open them," Dick urged and pushed the girls gently forward.

The guests had been instructed only to buy little presents as jokes and the girls were highly amused by the little green metal frog, intended as a paperweight, that croaked deeply when it was set down, the magnifying glass from Dick in memory of their detectiving, and all the other gifts.

Their present from Mavis was not, however, a joke like the others. The girls were speechless when they opened a large present and saw a brightly painted music box the lid of which had five holes carved out of it. Looking further among the tissue paper, they found five hand-carved wooden figures which fitted into the holes exactly. Each of the figures was about six inches tall. They all carried musical instruments and, they discovered, when the music box was wound up they revolved and seemed to be actually playing the tunes. There was a trumpet, a flute, an accordion, a snare drum, and a bass drum. The figures had been carved in almost lifelike positions. The trumpeter pointed his horn up into the air, while the flutist cocked his head in playing position. One could almost hear the roll of drumbeats as the figure holding the snare drum touched the instrument with his miniature sticks. Like the music box itself, each figure was gaily painted. They all wore high hats with small brims, tightly fitting red jackets with shiny gold epaulets, and blue trousers.

It was, in all, a beautiful work of art. "We've never had anything so lovely. Thank you, thank you, Mavis." Jo and Patty flung their arms about her neck.

"Ouch!" Mavis exclaimed, trying to disentangle herself from their enthusiastic embrace. "Let go of me before you choke me to death." The twins obediently released her. "I'll tell you a little story about this music box."

Everyone turned to listen and Mavis began: "When I was in Europe with the Red Cross, I was sent to Italy to do several months' work in a small town in the northern part. When I first arrived there, I decided to do some exploring to sort of get the feel of the town. Well, when I started out it was a beautiful day, but later it began to rain very hard. I couldn't get back to the room where I was staying without getting drenched. Instead, I ran up on the doorstep of a small shop and the kind proprietor insisted that I come inside to dry off a little.

"The downpour continued for an hour without a letup, so I had plenty of time to wander about the shop. There wasn't much for sale, for it had been a gift shop for tourists prior to the war. Of course, there weren't many trinkets and souvenirs being made then. But on a dusty shelf near the rear of the store I spied this music box and fell in love with it. It came to be one of my favorite possessions and I took it with me wherever I was sent after that. There were times when I had to leave something behind, since we always had to carry our own luggage. But the gay tunes the music box played when I was alone compensated for the difficulties I sometimes had in transporting it.

"You'll find that if you play it whenever you're feeling blue, those little figures will cheer you up in no time. I don't mean, of course, that I think you'll need cheering up often. I hope you'll get as much pleasure from it as I did."

"I'm sure we will." Jo wound the key at the side, pushed the lever and a tune started. Sure enough, the musical figures began to twirl around in time to the music.

Patty suddenly laughed aloud, pointing her finger at the bass drummer. He was, indeed, a comical sight. He was a rotund little man who leaned far back with his drum stretching upward. One of his short legs was lifted as though he was preparing to march smartly and one pudgy arm was stretched out from his side, the hand clutching a drumstick.

Jo giggled. "He does look funny, Patty, My, look how his head doesn't even reach the top of the drum! If he were real, he wouldn't be able to see

where he was going. Oh, and see how the little
accordion player holds his instrument stretched
way out. It's hard to decide which one I like
best."

"And the music box plays such gay, happy
tunes," Patty added. "They make me want to
dance." She seized Jo by the hands and twirled
her about. Breathless in a few minutes, they
turned back to watch again.

The rest of the guests gathered around and
everyone murmured in admiration.

While the party had been watching the music
box, Welton had slipped in with a large box.
Dick had seen him and said, as the music box
died down, "There's one package left here. You
forgot to open it."

But before either Patty or Jo could get to the
package, it opened itself! There, before their
eyes, stood a lively, brown, furry puppy wagging
his tail with delight. Around his neck was an
enormous bow of ribbon and a tag hung down
from it. The twins both made a dash for the
puppy at the same moment which startled the
dog. He leaped over their heads as they fell to

the floor in a heap and stood in the middle of the floor. There he taunted them with sharp yips. One was inclined to think he knew that he had fooled them.

At last Patty caught him in her arms and, while the puppy struggled, she managed to read the card. "Oh, Welty, he's precious. We never were able to have a dog before and how we've wanted one!" The puppy freed himself and started to lick Pat's face. She squealed and pushed him from her playfully.

Jo laughed at the sight and said, shaking her finger at the dog, "We'll have to teach you better manners, I can see that."

Just then Yamoto reappeared to announce that supper was ready, so the twins asked him to take the puppy into the back hall until after the party.

After a delicious supper the guests returned to the living room. Welton chose a variety of dance tunes from a pile of records and started the phonograph. Various couples began dancing, George Anderson claiming Pat for his partner.

"I'm the kind of guy who usually avoids parties," he said while they danced, "but this is one of the jolliest ever and I'm glad I came." He laughed. "I'm a pretty poor liar, but when I smell a party invitation, I can think up excuses by the dozens. Ask Elaine if you don't believe me."

Another record began to spin and Jo danced by on Dick's arm. "He seems to be partial to your sister, I've noticed," George commented. "That's the third dance in a row they've had together."

"Jo doesn't exactly hate him, either," laughed Pat. "I might add, though, that they do have heated arguments, sometimes. My sister is hot-tempered you'll find."

"That should do Dick some good. He's inclined to think his opinion is the only right opinion at times."

The music stopped and Dick and Jo edged over toward the door leading to the porch. Welton moved to the phonograph and reversed the records. As the music resumed, Jo protested she was too tired to dance any more.

"Let's go out on the porch then," Dick suggested. "I could stand a little fresh air."

Yamoto had even decorated the porch in honor of the girls' party. Jo hadn't noticed it in the dusk when they returned home, but now she gave a little exclamation of delight. Scallops of crepe paper edged the roof, giving the illusion of a tent, and small colored spotlights scattered among the shrubbery made a pattern of color on the floor.

"I must find Yamoto and tell him how nice it is," Jo announced when Dick told her whose handiwork it was. "Excuse me for a minute."

"Hold on, Jo, I want to talk to you. Yamoto will wait." He gently steered her over to the railing. "Look, I didn't want all of the others around when I gave you this. I—it's something just between us, you see."

While he was explaining Dick offered her a small white box. In it was a silver bracelet from which dangled a tiny silver heart engraved with her initials.

"Oh, Dick, it's perfectly beautiful." Jo's eyes were shining and her heart was beating fast.

"Turn it over," Dick directed.

So doing she discovered that on the reverse side of the heart had been engraved the initials "R. H. P."

"You'll be going off to college this fall and I'll be going back, too, of course. And gosh knows how long it will be before we see each other again. So—well—think of me if you wear it sometimes, will you do that for me, Jo?" He gazed at her earnestly. "You're—I think you're pretty much all right."

"I guess I'm pretty fond of you, too, Dick. And of course I'll wear it," she finished softly.

Jo smiled up into his eyes, and he bent down and kissed her tenderly. He held her for a moment, then let her go. Happier than she had ever been, Jo stood silently where she was. "My first real kiss," she thought over and over to herself, "my first real, grown-up kiss."

A sudden shout of laughter from indoors brought Jo out of her thoughts. "Even if I'm in love, I still must help look after our guests," she told herself. Then, aloud she said, "Come on, Dick, we'd better go inside."

Pat had noticed Dick take Jo outside and noticed, also, that her sister was glowing when they returned. She said nothing about it, however, but hoped Jo would tell her later. "We have no secrets from each other," she scolded herself for her selfish thoughts. "What's the matter with me, anyway?"

The party broke up around midnight. Calling goodnight and more birthday wishes back and forth between the drive and the porch, the guests departed. Welton went around the house to make sure the lights were turned off and the doors locked. By the time he had finished, the rest of the household was making ready to go to bed.

Before going into her own room, Mavis looked in on the twins. At the moment when she appeared in the doorway, Jo had finished telling Pat about her gift from Dick and was putting it back into its box. "Oh, Mavis, look!" she cried, drawing the bracelet out again. And then she told her story all over. "It was a grand party, Mavis. You and Welty have done so much for us."

Welton, too, was attracted to the room by the sound of voices. He heard the end of Jo's conversation and replied, "Why, my dear, why shouldn't we do things for you? You're like our own daughters, you know."

Pat had been sitting quietly on her bed all this while. Finally, not able to meet their eyes, she murmured in a low voice, "And yesterday I was complaining to Jo that nobody had remembered our birthday. I owe you both an apology for the unkind thoughts I had."

Mavis came around her bed and sat down beside her. "I thought you were glum this morning. Darling, don't ever be afraid we'll forget about you. Why, we're the fortunate ones, please try to remember that, always." She kissed her affectionately and squeezed her hand. "Now, get into bed as fast as you can. It's awfully late." She rose and left the room with Welton, who blew them each a kiss and closed the door softly.

It was a long time before the girls were able to settle down and go to sleep. Twice they had to turn the light back on to see if their music box was still on the chest beside the window. They even got out of bed and examined the figures more closely. On an impulse Jo nearly wound the key at the side, but Patty put out a restraining hand. It would not do to arouse the entire household, she reminded her sister. They lay awake and talked together long after the house was quiet, but at last they fell asleep.

Long past their usual waking hour, Pat opened her eyes and looked at the clock on the night table which stood between their beds.

"Great heavens, Jo!" she cried, shaking her twin vigorously. "Look at the time. It's ten-thirty!"

"Hnh? What?" came a drowsy answer. Jo rolled over and pulled the sheet over her head.

Pat jumped out of bed and slipped into her robe. A few moments later Jo heard her splashing in the bathroom and groaned. When Pat returned she dressed quickly and as she left again, Jo mumbled something inaudible.

"What'd you say?" Pat playfully drew the sheet back.

"I said you can bring me my breakfast in bed." Jo tugged at the sheet and pulled it back over her head.

"Not on your life, lazybones! Besides, Mrs. Gruber wouldn't stand for it." Pat sailed out of the door in search of Mrs. Gruber and breakfast.

"Good morning, Mrs. Gruber. Where is everybody?" Pat opened the refrigerator and found two glasses of orange juice. She took one of them.

"Morning, Patricia. Mrs. Duer, she's out in the garden. I expect Mr. Duer's working in his study as usual. Fine time to be getting up in the morning. Where's your sister?"

"Gosh, I'm sorry, honestly. We must have overslept. Here, give me those eggs. I can fix our breakfast. You must be awfully busy."

Mrs. Gruber willingly handed her the eggs and said, "Well, there is a lot of work to be done. Cleaning up after your party and all that. My stars! It seems as though a body works and works cleaning and cooking for a special shindig and then, soon's it's over, you spend twice as much time cleaning up *after* it." All the while she was talking Mrs. Gruber was taking things out of the cleaning closet. Rags, mops, pails, vacuum cleaner appeared behind her and punctuated each statement. When she had removed everything she wanted from the closet, she piled them into her arms and, pushing the vacuum along in front of her, she strode into the living room.

"Poor thing," Pat said softly, "I'll bet she doesn't like the change in her life since we kids came into it."

The eggs were sputtering in the pan and the bacon was done and draining when Jo wandered into the kitchen, yawning. "Something smells good. Umm, bacon and eggs. Boy, is Mrs. Gruber grouchy this morning! I said good morning to her, but she just grunted and glared at me."

"We'd better keep out of her way today. I don't think she likes parties very much, Jo. She gave me a long lecture about them." She giggled and handed Jo two loaded plates. "Here, if you'll take these, I'll bring the coffee."

Just then the back door flew open and Mavis came in. She was wearing a floppy straw sun hat and a pair of bulky work gloves. These she drew off her hands and laid on the kitchen table.

"Hi, you two. Did you sleep well? My, I'm a sight!" She leaned over the small mirror that hung beside the sink. Her face was streaked with dirt and several locks of hair had escaped from under her hat. "I've been weeding. I never dreamed there could be so many weeds!" She turned on the faucet and washed her hands and face.

"We'll help you after we've had our breakfast," Pat offered. She held the door for Mavis, then followed her into the dining room.

"Join us for some coffee," Jo urged.

Mavis sat down and gratefully accepted a cup. Jo chuckled, her head buried in the morning newspaper.

"It isn't very polite to read at the table," Pat protested. "Or, if you insist on doing it, you might at least tell us what's so funny."

"Just the comics," Jo murmured. She shoved

them toward her sister. "Here, I'm finished. Want 'em?"

"No, thank you," came a prim answer.

A chair scraped back as Jo stood up suddenly. "Say, I almost forgot! Where's our pup?"

"He was out in the garden with us," Mavis answered. "You should have seen him racing back and forth shaking an old glove Welty had found for him. It finally got to be too much for Yamoto. He was so worried that the dog would ruin some of the flowers. He put him in the drying yard back of the tool shed and closed the gate. He should still be there."

"We'll have to think up a good name for him," Pat said, munching a piece of toast and looking up at her sister. "We can't just call him 'puppy.'"

"Let's call him Lucky, because that's how we felt last night when we saw him, wasn't it?"

"A perfect name, Jo. Do you like it, Mavis?" Mavis nodded, smiling. "Lucky, he is, then."

The telephone began to ring in the hall and Mavis started to rise to answer it, but sat down again when she heard Mrs. Gruber switch off the vacuum. They heard her answer and a moment later she came in.

"For you, Patricia. It's that young man again. He called while you were still in bed."

"Thanks." Pat excused herself and went into the hall. "Hello? . . . Oh, George, it's you." She laughed, then listened. "Yes . . . yes, sure . . . wait a minute until I ask Jo." She laid down the phone and returned to the dining table. "It's George," she reported to Jo, "he wants to know would we like some tennis this afternoon. Want to play? Dick's coming, too."

"Sure. Tell him the girls will play against the boys—and beat 'em, too!"

The days seemed to fly by for the Faraday twins. There was so much that interested them. They joined in swimming parties, tennis and moonlight picnics on the beach. Then they had their work with Welton and gardening with Yamoto and Mavis. Jo was becoming quite an expert gardener according to Yamoto who was an expert one himself, and so this was high praise.

Lucky was growing day by day until the girls wondered if he would ever stop. They took great delight in training him to do tricks, such as to roll over and to sit up and beg. He proved to be fond of the water, also, and often, of his own accord, would paddle about in the lake. Many a sun bath was disrupted when he came too near, shaking the water from his coat.

True to her word, Jo did try to teach Lucky proper manners. He followed them in to lunch one day and Jo scolded him for it. "Dogs don't belong in the dining room when we're eating, Lucky. Go 'way. No one is going to feed you anything here."

Pat diverted Jo's attention with a question concerning the afternoon's plans and Welton chose that moment to surreptitiously feed Lucky a choice morsel from his plate.

But he was too slow to escape Jo's alert eyes. "Oh, no, you don't, Welty. You can't get away with that. I saw you!" She pointed an accusing finger at him.

Welton laughed and his face reddened. "I was only teasing you, Jo. I wasn't really going to give it to him."

"I wondered," Pat mused, "why Lucky was getting so fat. He seemed to be getting plenty of exercise. So you're the culprit!"

"Oh, Mavis," Jo interrupted, "when Elaine was

over this morning she asked us to play our music box and there seems to be something wrong with it. One of the figures doesn't twirl around properly. I feel utterly dismal about it. Is there anything you can do?"

"Why, that's a shame, Jo. I'll look at it, but I'm no mechanic."

Jo looked gloomy.

"Perhaps Yamoto will know what to do," Mavis added hastily. "And, if not, we'll send it to an expert repairman."

"Hello, everyone. Invite me to lunch." The informal order came from Dick, who had stopped in on his way home from his lifeguard duties on the beach. Without receiving the invitation he had asked for he drew a chair up to the table and waited, grinning.

Jo found a particularly interesting spot on the ceiling and, gazing at it intently, she said, "Speaking of dogs and their training and we were a moment ago, I wonder who trained the one on my left."

Assuming an injured air, Dick jumped to his feet and said, "Very well, if you'd rather I left . . ."

"Do stay," urged Mavis, putting her hand on

his arm. The door behind her opened and she turned at the sound. "Oh, Yamoto, is there enough for one more? Dick's staying."

"Always plenty for one more. I bring plate," he replied.

"Say, Welty, old man," Dick said, addressing his friend, "do you know who I ran into on my way up the cliff? Old Mr. Daniels, remember him? He owns that huge place on Mountain Road," he said in explanation to the girls. "He hasn't been living in it for several years."

"I remember him well," Welton replied. "We used to do a lot of fishing together. A fine old gentleman and a great sportsman. Let me see now, it seems he moved West when he left here. Oregon, wasn't it?"

"Right. And believe it or not, he said he came back this year because he's missed the fishing. I thought Oregon had streams superior to ours, but he claims they aren't. He asked if you still lived here and when I said you did, he said to tell you he just spent a week fishing up along Spruce Creek. Says he had marvelous luck."

"You don't say? Well, now, that's an interesting piece of news."

"Golly, Welty, remember the good times we've had together fishing in that old creek? I guess you taught me just about all I know about fishing."

Yamoto re-entered with the main course. He moved about the table setting the steaming plates of food down before each place. Pat reached for the bread plate, then passed it on to Dick.

Stuffing a piece in his mouth, he said, "We haven't fished together even once this summer, Welty. Do you realize that?" He chewed reflectively.

"I'm not as free to come and go as I please, my boy." Welton winked at him. "I've got a houseful of women who are forever planning my social calendar for me. No," he sighed with mock wistfulness, "I'm afraid those carefree days are over for me."

Mavis laughed. "We'll let you go fishing, dear . . ."

"You will?"

"Provided you take us with you," she finished.

"Girls don't belong on a fishing trip," Dick objected.

"Ugh, who cares?" came from Jo.

"Oh, a sissy, eh? Afraid to bait a hook, I'll bet."

"No, that part I don't mind. It's taking the fish off the hook while it's still wriggling that I don't like."

"Go on, you'd be lucky to get that far!"

Welton laid down his fork and wiped his mouth with his napkin. Looking across the table at his wife, he said, "Seriously, though, Dick's got me to thinking about this. I think a little fishing trip, all of us together, would be a nice outing. What do you think, my dear?"

"It's a splendid idea, sweet. You have been working awfully hard and a few days' rest would do you good."

"Fine, we'll all go. Dick, you'll come, of course. Patty, Jo, would you like a little trip up north of here? You needn't fish if it's distasteful to you."

"Jo doesn't really know what she's talking about," Pat insisted. "She's never fished and neither have I. We'd love to try it, wouldn't we?" She turned to her sister, who nodded in agreement.

"We can leave Yamoto in charge here, and perhaps Mrs. Gruber would enjoy a few days off," Welton continued, planning ahead in his mind.

"Mrs. Gruber mentioned to me just yesterday

that she wished to visit a sister of hers in May-
ville. I know she'll be pleased," Mavis returned.

"Do you think you could arrange everything
so that we could leave, say, early next week?"

"Oh, yes, if you'll take care of your fishing gear
and tents, I can manage the food and clothes."

And so it was decided that they would have a
week of camping and fishing. The rest of the
week was a busy one for the entire household.
Welton spent a great deal of time sorting over
his fishing tackle, which he had not examined
since the previous summer. Jo and Patty helped
him in dusting off the creels, rewinding lines and
arranging the colorful lures and flies. During
these sessions both of the girls asked innumerable
questions concerning the use of the various pieces
of equipment.

When it came to the camping gear the twins
knew nearly as much as Welton did about it. The
times they had spent with their father had been
mainly a series of camps. Bedrolls, ponchos and
mess kits were very familiar to them.

Dick came nearly every day to compare notes
with Welton on fishing tackle and whether it was

advisable to try some new scheme of casting that he had read or heard about.

Meanwhile Mavis was occupied in planning what sort of food to take with them and checking over the family wardrobes.

The preparation seemed endless to Patty and Jo, but miraculously enough by the end of the week everything was assembled and ready.

5   *"Water, Water, Everywhere . . ."*

ALTHOUGH AN early start had been planned for the morning that the fishing party was to get under way, as always happens not enough time nor space was allowed for stowing the camping equipment in the station wagon. Such delays annoyed and flustered Welton, but Dick and Yamoto managed most of the packing. There was really little cause for his muddled frame of mind. At last, however, after eliminating a few bulky

packages of geology equipment that he had insisted he needed, they were ready to go.

"This is a vacation, dear, not an archeological
expedition," Mavis reminded him.

"I know, I know, but you never know where
you may find a valuable bit of information. I like
to be prepared, my dear."

"Go on, Welty," Dick cajoled him, "you've been
over every inch of that part of the state. You know
exactly what it holds—ahem—geologically speaking, you might say. Where are the twins?"

"They went to tie up Lucky. They were afraid
he might try to follow them," Mavis told him.

"Well, whenever those women choose to put
in an appearance, *we're* ready to go," he stated
impatiently.

Mrs. Gruber came down the steps carrying her
suitcase. "Oh, no!" Dick wailed. "Not something
more to find space for." He collapsed into a lawn
chair, throwing up his hands in despair.

"Don't worry, Dick, she's only going with us as
far as the village. She's taking the bus from there."
Mavis tried to soothe him.

"Well, okay, then, but you'll probably have to

balance it on your head, Mrs. Gruber. I don't know where else to put it."

At this Mrs. Gruber found she was laughing in spite of herself.

Presently Patty and Jo rounded the corner of the house. Fortunately they came empty-handed.

"Are we ever going to get started?" Patty called. "We've been ready for simply ages."

"We've been waiting for you slowpokes," Dick retorted.

They drove perhaps seventy-five miles northward to reach Spruce Creek. The sky was overcast and a gray pall covered the countryside. It was a strange day for midsummer; rain threatened but did not come. The party speeding along the highway saw groups of cattle huddled together which they interpreted as a sure sign of a storm. In spite of the fact that all of the windows were rolled down as far as they would go, it was stuffy and close in the car. The three young people shared the rear seat while Welton and Mavis rode in front.

Mavis anxiously scanned the lowering sky. "I only wish it would rain now and get it over with. It's so unpleasant to camp when your clothes and

tent gear are soggy." She was an experienced outdoors woman and more than once had weathered
fierce storms. Her talk, therefore, was not idle.

"I think we have a chance to move away from
the storm area. I checked the weather map in the
newspaper last night and it looked as though the
storm center was moving south." Welton peered
ahead along the highway.

"This may ruin our fishing for a day or so," Dick
mourned.

"Why, Dick?" Pat asked. Fishing was one sport
with which she was unfamiliar, although both she
and Jo excelled in most sports.

"Fish swim at the bottom of the stream, river
or lake when it's raining. That's because the rain
muddies the water, which they don't like, and
they don't come near the surface to feed."

"Then, even after the weather clears, it would
be some time before the fishing conditions were
favorable again, is that right?" Jo reasoned.

"Yes, some time after the weather clears the
fish again swim near the surface," Dick affirmed.
"Not even the most experienced fisherman can
say exactly when. Fish are pretty unpredictable
creatures—like women!"

He was in danger of losing his seat at this last remark, as both girls lunged for him. Welton helped them unknowingly, for he made a sharp turn-off to the left, which led them onto a bumpy, narrow dirt road. The hard jolt as the car shifted from the smooth asphalt highway to the unpaved road threw the three in the back seat together.

"I would have warned you about that turn if you hadn't been going to push me off, anyway," laughed Dick when they had untangled themselves. "That marks the beginning of the end of our ride."

Tree branches brushed the side of the car as it wove its way along, following ruts that had formed over years of infrequent but regular travel. A mile or so back from the main highway, Welton brought the car to a stop.

"We'll do the rest of the trip to our camping site on foot," he said. "Dick, let's take only the tents and cooking utensils this first trip. You and I can come back for the rest after we've set up the tents."

Welton and Dick sorted out the things they planned to take and handed some of them to Mavis and the girls. Each one carried his own bedroll, which made it easier. When everything was distributed the party set out.

As they left the car Mavis again looked up at the sky. "Those black clouds to the east are moving this way, Welton," she said in a worried tone of voice.

"Don't worry, my dear, we haven't far to go and we will have these tents up in a jiffy."

Dick led the way along a narrow, winding trail that presently diminished altogether. Jo followed him, then came Mavis and Pat, with Welton bringing up the rear. A dense undergrowth hampered their progress already slowed by their packs.

"How do you know where you're going, Dick? The path's gone," Jo asked. Then she answered her own question. "Oh, there's a trail blazed, isn't there? I just noticed."

A few moments later Pat's muffled voice drifted to the front of the group from behind the bundle she was carrying. "Is it much farther?" She paused for a moment to rest. The air was really stifling in the dense woods and the bulky package made her even hotter.

Welton caught up with her and encouraged

her to continue. "It's only a few steps now, Patty girl."

Sure enough, a clearing revealed itself through the tangled trees. When they emerged from the woods into the clearing a rushing, tumbling brook greeted their eyes and even their ears. A small falls directly before them caused the noise. From the falls the water coursed along for a space of fifty feet and then the stream widened and the water moved more slowly.

Setting her bundle down and slipping the straps of the bedroll from her shoulders, Pat walked over and joined the others at the edge of the stream. She plunged her hands up to her wrists into the cool water and let them remain there for a few minutes. Then, she splashed some on her face and felt at once refreshed.

Dick and Welton went off again to cut tent poles, while the remaining three busied themselves untying bundles. As soon as the men returned they started to raise the tents.

Jo and Patty volunteered to collect firewood against the oncoming storm and went off together. Mavis stayed behind to give Welton and Dick help in raising the tents. Everyone hurried against time, so that few words were spoken except to give a brief direction.

When Jo and Patty returned to the camp site, the men were gone on another trip to the car and the tents, two of them, were up. Mavis's head poked out from one of them as the girls approached.

"My, what a load of firewood!" she called when they were within earshot.

"It should last a while, shouldn't it?" Jo called back to her. She was dragging a huge limb behind her in addition to holding a bundle of kindling crooked in her arm. Pat was equally laden.

"Let's put them in one of the tents, so they will stay dry," Mavis suggested as she ran up to meet them. She took some wood from each girl.

No sooner had they finished piling the wood when a loud tattoo began on the canvas roof.

"Here it comes!" Jo shouted above the din.

"Oh, dear," wailed Mavis, "the boys will be soaked. I do hope they reached the car and have sense enough to stay there until this stops."

The rain continued to pour, with an occasional clap of thunder and flashes of lightning. Watching the storm rage from the tent flap, the three huddled together. Now and then a gust of wind whipped the rain into their faces. When this happened, they quickly closed the flap, but the stale air which collected in a few moments forced them to open it again.

It was almost pitch black outside. Once in a while a flash of lightning revealed the banks of the stream in an eerie, pale green light. The wind roared endlessly in the trees overhead. Eventually the rain was reduced to a light, steady drizzle and not too many minutes later, Pat spied Dick and Welton running toward them from the edge of the clearing. Each carried a bundle wrapped in a tarpaulin and swung a suitcase in one hand. They dashed into the tent where they stood for a moment, breathing heavily.

"Made it," puffed Dick at last.

"Whew," sighed Welton, then he laughed. "I'm certainly out of condition. I used to be able to outrun you, Dick."

Dick grinned. He made a circle of his fingers and ran them down his bare arms in order to remove some of the water. Rain dripped from his hair and the cuffs of his heavy duck pants were brimming over.

"Goodness! You're both drenched!" Mavis exclaimed. "Why didn't you wait until this storm was over?"

"Gee, this isn't going to stop today," Dick stated. "It's settling down to an all-night drizzle, if I don't miss my guess."

"Yes, dear, I'm afraid he's right. Good, I see you gathered a fine pile of wood, girls. Now don't tell me you carried that huge log yourselves!" he added, walking around the stack and spying the limb.

"I just dragged it, Welty."

"Humph. Looks like something a cat wouldn't drag in," Dick joked.

Dick's spirits were not dampened by mere weather. He was always good-natured and ready for fun. He made a fine addition to any group and Patty and Jo were glad he was with them now, even though his jokes were sometimes at their expense.

A fire was started with some difficulty, but it was not hard to keep it going once the dry branches and twigs caught. Soon hamburger patties were frying and Pat sat toasting buns speared with a stick, one of the tarpaulins draped over her head. A pot of coffee struggled to perk against the rain. Soon the meal was ready and, after eating heartily, the group agreed that they might as well turn in for the night.

The next day dawned bright and clear. Patty and Jo awoke to hear the birds chirping loudly, and they knew immediately that the rain had stopped. When they stepped out into the bright sunshine they found that the ground was still damp and soggy.

"Will we fish today?" Pat asked eagerly as the party cleared up the remains of breakfast.

"Well, we'll try our luck, anyway," asserted Welton. He and Dick had been up ahead of the others and had already made a trip back to the car for the remainder of their equipment which included the fishing tackle. Now he was busy assembling rods.

A short time later the group could be found strung out several yards apart along the stream some distance above the camp site. Getting the twins acquainted with the fundamentals of fly fishing had kept their minds off the fact that the fish weren't biting that morning.

Welton handed an assembled rod to each of

the girls, explaining, "These are some old poles of mine you can practice with. If, later on, you find you like the sport, we'll see that you have your own equipment."

Jo was watching Dick make a practice cast and tried to imitate his style. She held the pole vertically, as he had done, then moved it into a horizontal position. She looked into the stream but saw no line. Turning around she found that her line had become hopelessly tangled in the bushes. Dick, looking on, ran over, laughing, and helped her to untangle the mess.

As he rewound the line around the reel he said, "Here, let me show you how."

He handed back the rod to her and placed her right hand in the correct position at the end of the rod. "Now," he directed, "reel out some of your line. Not too much, there. Okay, listen carefully. When you bring the rod up over your head, you have to flex your wrist quickly. If you do it right, the line will snap straight into the water. Got it?"

Jo puckered her lips in concentration. "I think so," she said briefly.

"Try it, then."

It was better than her first try, but the hook caught in the grassy bank in front of her. Dick walked over and disengaged it.

"Stand a little closer to the edge, Jo. I think you're too far away."

Her next cast was successful. The lure bobbed on the surface of the water and, following Dick's instruction, she slowly reeled in her line.

"If you feel a tug on your line, let it out a little —not too much or you'll lose your fish."

Pat was receiving similar directions from Welton with Mavis looking on. It may have been because she had two instructors or perhaps it was just beginner's luck, but, whatever the reason, she was the first to feel a nibble.

"I think I've got something!" she said tensely.

The tautness of her line indicated she was right. "Play out your line a bit, Pat," Welton ordered. "Let the fish tire itself out before you reel it in. It's a sure way to snap your line, if you jerk it in too fast."

Pat tried her best to follow his advice, but the fish was very strong. It darted this way and that, trying to rid itself of the hook.

"I'm slipping!" she cried.

Welton tossed his own pole to the ground and rushed to her side. But it was too late. Patty slid from the bank into the shallow water, losing the pole in the descent.

"The rod," she wailed, "it's sailing down the creek!"

Dick, hearing her, looked up in time to see the rod approaching him. He waded out into the stream in his high rubber boots and snatched it. He scrambled up the bank again, muddying his shirt sleeve. His contact with the muddy bank was not nearly so extensive as Pat's, he saw when he returned the rod. The back of her slacks, the back of her blouse, and one sleeve where she had tried to brace herself were covered with a sticky layer of mud. She was, indeed, a sight.

She stood up, trying to pick off some of the mud when Dick approached. He couldn't keep from grinning at her, but he said, "Let it dry first, Patsy, then it will brush right off."

"Ugh! I feel clammy," she shuddered, then giggled. "Am I a confirmed fisherman, now?"

"You're baptized, all right," Dick quipped.

No one else felt a nibble on his line all morning. Jo thought she had something once, only to discover that she had caught a snag. When the shadows cast into the water by the overhanging trees had become dwarfed in size, the fishing party recessed for lunch. Grilled cheese sandwiches replaced fish on the menu. The morning's fishing was discussed over and over until Mavis declared that the twins were talking like veterans.

It continued to rain intermittently during the rest of their trip, but they did manage to catch a few fish and had a delicious supper of them. At last, one morning Welton announced that he didn't see any point in trying to fish under such unfavorable conditions and he, for one, was in favor of a day's hike instead.

"Count us in," chorused Patty and Jo.

"Not me," said Dick flatly. "I came here to fish and fish I will. When you get back, hot and tired and hungry from your tramp, *I'll* have a mess of fish sizzling in the pan."

Mavis decided to stay behind, too, promising to have something equally delicious ready, in case Dick could not live up to his boasts.

"We'll get some grub together, Welty, and we can hike all day," Patty said.

In a few minutes they were on their way.

Welton had decided that, since they were in the vicinity, it was a good chance to show the girls a state park which, he hinted darkly, was a mysterious place. Since it was ten miles distant they took the car.

Soon after they were back on the highway once again, Welton slowed the car at the park entrance. It was, Jo observed as she read aloud from the sign to the right of the entrance, LOST LAKE VISITORS WELCOME STATE PARK. The other two smiled in amusement as Jo deliberately misread the message on the sign.

"Silly way to write a sign, I must say," Jo commented. "Seriously, what do they mean, Welty, is the lake really lost?"

"That's what we came to find out," was the mysterious answer.

The guard at the entrance waved them into a large parking space. The tires crunched in the loose gravel of the lot. The few cars already parked indicated they would not be bothered by many fellow trampers.

"I don't think we'll need to roll up the windows, Pat," Welton said as he saw her put her hand on the lever. "It surely can't rain any more. Can you reach the lunch? Hand it to me then. Now, follow me."

There were several paths leading from the parking lot. The one Welton chose went downhill for several hundred yards. Then, as the terrain leveled, the path ended.

"In this park," Welton explained to the girls, "there are only a few trails marked. The park commissioners realized when they planned this area that many people prefer to strike out on their own. Since there are no wild animals there is little real danger and, besides, the park is well-patrolled by members of the park police force."

"Can't you tell us now what we are going to look for?" Pat asked curiously.

"Remember that first hike we took in our own woods when I told you about the river?"

The twins nodded. Of course they remembered. "You said sometimes a river would change its course," Jo reminded him.

"That's right, a river always seeks the lowest level. You asked a few moments ago if the lake was really lost that gives the park its name. Look ahead there." He pointed in the direction of a clearing ahead and below the place where they were standing.

"All I can see is a plain old field," Pat said.

"What's that got to do with it?" Jo asked.

"Quite a good deal. I'll give you a clue. As we go down that hill ahead of us, which leads into the field, look carefully at the hill itself."

The girls followed him down. About halfway to the bottom, Pat exclaimed, "Golly, it certainly is hard to keep your footing. It's so sandy along here."

"I see some rocks down there. Look like the sandstone you were telling us about, Welty." This came from Jo.

"Uh-huh," was all that Duer would say in reply.

At last they reached the bottom of the hill and found themselves on the edge of the field. To the west a valley provided the only way out of the depression between the surrounding hills.

"You've proved to be good observers. You noticed the soil was sandy and that there was some sandstone underneath which showed where the soil had eroded away from it."

"Did we say all that?" Jo asked, and both girls laughed.

"Well, perhaps not in precisely those words," chuckled Welton. "Now, do you remember the floods we talked about?" Both girls nodded.

"That is exactly what happened here. Thousands of years ago a river flowed through that valley and emptied into this field. Then floods came and the river churned and the waters roared over the banks. Trees crashing down, huge chunks of earth were moved until the terrain was changed considerably. Finally, when the waters receded, the river found it could no longer flow along its old bed. It had raised the banks so high near its mouth that it could not get to the lake.

"But, as I have pointed out to you before, the river was pretty clever and if it was unable to flow one way, why, it would just go elsewhere. In short, it changed its course. Then, since the lake here was no longer fed by water from the river, it gradually dried up."

"But how do you know all this? Wouldn't it have been just as likely for the same thing to happen in another way? I was thinking of the glaciers that once covered this part of the world," Pat explained.

"That's a good question. However, if that had happened, we would have found lots of huge boulders and stones here that would likely be granite or quartz. What I mean is, they would be rocks that would not have matched the other rocks of the region. You see, the glaciers were so powerful that they moved rocks and earth great distances. They account for the rocky terrain in New England, which is quite different from this region."

"Then it must be possible for you to tell just about everything that ever happened on earth," Jo commented, her eyes wide with wonderment.

"Not quite," Welton laughed. "There are still many, many things we have yet to find the answer for. Remember that this earth of ours is billions of years old."

"This seems a lovely place for lunch," Pat hinted not too obscurely. They had eaten breakfast earlier than usual that morning and it was now past noon. The sun was high in the sky overhead.

"A splendid idea, Patsy my girl," Welton replied with enthusiasm. "It seems that when I get wound up on my favorite subject, I just don't know when to stop."

Jo and Patty proceeded to unpack the basket they had brought. Jo spread the tablecloth out on the soft grass and put three paper plates on top of it. A brief gust of wind caught the corner of the cloth and scattered the plates. Pat scrambled after one of them which, because of its lightness, had blown some distance away. Jo plunked a sandwich down on each of the plates to guard against further mishap.

"I think it would be better if we each hold our own cup of milk. Here's yours, Welty. Steady, Pat, you're spilling that stuff all over my hand."

At the end of the meal Jo groaned, but it was a contented groan. She stretched out on the grass and blinked her eyes against the bright sunlight. "I don't know why I ate so much. Now I could go right to sleep."

"Too bad you're so greedy," Patty reminded her. She, too, really felt a little uncomfortable from the three huge sandwiches she had put away. This she would not have admitted to Jo, however.

"I didn't notice you starving yourself, exactly,"

was Jo's quick reply. "If you feel so energetic, why don't you clean up this debris?"

Pat went over and tickled her twin. Not until Jo yelled for mercy would she stop. "Get up and help me then," she laughed. Brushing herself off Jo rose to a sitting position. She leaned over and started crumpling paper plates and napkins and stuffed them into the basket.

Welton, meanwhile, had wandered off to some distance away from the girls and stood gazing about him and smoking his pipe. The sound of the laughing girls pleased him. He liked the way they got along with each other with hardly any bickering between them. He concluded that they were exceptional and congratulated himself for the decision he had made regarding them. He turned and walked back to the picnic site.

"Where to now, Welty?" Jo asked. The feeling of drowsiness had left her.

"Would you like to walk a little way up that valley? I don't know just where it leads, but if I remember correctly, it winds about until it reaches the main highway only a quarter of a mile from the park entrance.

"That suits me. How about you, Jo?"

Jo agreed and struck off ahead of the others. Welty followed her and Pat hesitated a moment, making sure that they had left no papers to disfigure the landscape. Her years of camping with their father had trained her to dislike a disorderly camping ground. Welton and Jo were far ahead of her as she hurried to catch up with them.

Suddenly Jo heard a crash. Turning quickly she saw Welton stop, turn and start to run back the way they had just come. Jo, too, broke into a run. Pat must have slipped on the stony trail!

6   A Thief and a Toy Drummer

LEONARDO HAD walked a long way and his shoes were dusty. He paused at the entrance to the driveway and took a handkerchief from his trouser pocket. First he carefully wiped the perspiration from his face, then he stooped and removed the dust from his shoes as best he could. His dark eyebrows met as he frowned at the scuff marks visible once the dust had been removed.

Sighing, he straightened his broad shoulders and replaced the handkerchief in the pocket of his ill-fitting suit. Leonardo looked again at the piece of paper he held clenched in one hand and verified the name and address. "Mavis Martin—no, I crossed that out—Mrs. Welton Duer," he read aloud, "Number 3 Crest Drive, Harker's Cove, Michigan." He glanced again at the two stone pillars on either side of the drive. One read Number 3, the other, Crest Drive.

"This must be it. The last chance," he whispered to himself.

He stuffed the paper into his pocket and held his hand there, two fingers tightly crossed. Superstitious? He wondered to himself. "I have reason to be." He quickened his steps as he neared the porch of the lodge.

He mounted the steps one at a time as if he wanted to delay a minute or two. In front of the door he looked around first for the doorbell, but, seeing none, he raised his fist and knocked softly. While he waited he gave his tie a tug to make sure it was straight. After a moment of silence he knocked again, this time more loudly. Still no answer. The third series of knocks was long and insistent.

Leonardo hated to leave but it seemed as

though there was nothing else for him to do. "Perhaps someone is in the back of the house and didn't hear me," he thought, grasping for a straw of hope. He retraced his steps to the driveway, then went around to the rear.

At the kitchen door he knocked again loudly several times, but no one came. Utterly discouraged he continued around the house the other way, instead of retracing his footsteps. He looked in at the low windows of the living room, hoping to see someone, anyone. Next he passed the window of the bedroom that Patty and Jo shared.

He looked in again, started to move on, when suddenly he saw something. Without thinking he moved closer to the window and tried to open it. It gave under the pressure of his strong hands.

Swiftly he opened it further and climbed in, his eyes staring fixedly ahead as though he was dazed. He made straight for the music box and picked up one of the little drummers. "This is the one, this is the one," he muttered over and over to himself.

What was that? Footsteps! "I've got to get out of here. I mustn't be found here!" Panic-stricken he fled still clutching the figure. Only when he was once more outside and had turned to close the window did he realize that he still held the drummer. There was no time to go back now. Instead, Leonardo closed the window as quietly as he could and crept away.

Yamoto had heard a noise when he returned from his trip to the woods with Lucky. Having extra time while the family was enjoying their fishing trip, he had taken the opportunity to chop logs which would be needed for the fireplace in the coming winter. Stopping to wipe his feet carefully before he went into the house, however, was long enough for the unexpected visitor to escape. As Yamoto made a swift check of the rooms he assured himself that he had only imagined the noise.

Satisfied, he went back out of doors and picked up his load of logs. Calling to Lucky, who came bounding toward him, he went out to the tool shed to add the wood he had chopped to what was already piled there. He opened the door, stepped inside and began methodically to arrange the logs. Lucky whined and sniffed.

"What's matteh, Lucky boy?" Yamoto looked puzzled, then his face brightened. "Yamoto not

shut you in? Not this tlime." He reached down
and patted the dog fondly.

If only Yamoto had investigated the tool shed,
he would have discovered a strange young man
cowering behind the door! Instead he finished his
task and left the shed, closing the door behind
him. His footsteps crunching on the graveled
driveway indicated to Leonardo that he was safe.

Now to get out of here, thought the boy. He
looked down at the wooden figure which lay in
his hand. "Why? oh, why did I take this?" he
whispered fiercely. "I should put it back, but
how?" He searched his mind wildly for some
scheme that he could use to return it.

If only he could get back to the road without
being seen, he could start all over again and
approach the house just as he had the first time.
"No," he thought, "that won't do, either. This
man, whoever he is, wouldn't let me inside. Besides, even if he did, he wouldn't leave me alone
so that I could put this back. And I can't just go
up to him and say, 'Pardon me, I found this and
I think it's yours.' I have what I came all this way
for, but now that I have it I'm not so sure I
want it."

He peeked out of the one small window in the tool shed and looked carefully in all directions. No one was in sight, not even the dog. He opened the door cautiously and looked out carefully again. He decided to make a break for the woods. He ran swiftly across the few yards of lawn which separated the tool shed from the edge of the woods.

Breathing heavily he leaned his head against a tree trunk behind a protective cover of undergrowth. He had not stopped running when he entered the woods, but had gone on until he could run no longer. The snapping of splitting twigs had filled his ears with noise until he wondered that no one had followed him, he had crashed about so. His breathing was regular now and he decided to walk on to his left. When he reached a spot that he hoped would be beyond the property on which he had trespassed, he would turn left again and perhaps reach the highway without further mishap.

Pat's eyes were closed when Welton reached her. He knelt beside her and reached for her wrist. With experienced fingers he felt for her pulse. He found it and assured himself that she was only temporarily stunned. A large lump was beginning to appear on her forehead.

Jo reached them and asked breathlessly what had happened.

"She must have tripped and fell, knocking her head against that low-hanging branch just back of where she's lying. I don't think she's hurt badly. There—she's opening her eyes."

Pat raised her hand to her forehead and rubbed the lump. She winced as she did so. "Clumsy of me, wasn't it?" She smiled weakly and tried to sit up.

"You'd better lie still for a minute or two, honey. Is it only your head that hurts?" Welton asked anxiously. Jo tenderly smoothed the hair back from Pat's forehead.

"I think so. I bumped into that tree in my haste. It must have knocked me out."

After a few minutes Pat again tried to sit up, this time successfully. She slowly rose to her feet with Welton and Jo supporting her on either side. Once on her feet she felt much better and the color returned to her pale cheeks.

"Try walking around a little," Welton directed.

"Hurt any place? No? Well, do you think you can make it back to the car?"

Pat bit her lips but she said she was only a little stiff and would be all right. Slowly they started out once more. A few yards further, Pat reached out for Welton's arm and leaned against him rather heavily. "My knee," she gasped, "I must have twisted it as I fell."

They stopped while she rolled up the leg of her slacks. Sure enough, the discolored area surrounding her knee showed signs of a severe bruise. Welton felt it with expert fingers.

"It's a nasty bruise all right, although I think that's the extent of it. At least I hope so."

"If you'll let me lean on you the rest of the way, Welty, I think I can make it. How far is it to the car?"

"About a mile, I'm afraid. I would suggest we go back the way we came, for it is shorter, really, but that steep hill would be even worse for you to climb. Go ahead, lean against my shoulder. That's the way."

Slowly, painfully, they walked the long distance to the parking lot. At times, Pat felt they would never get there. Then, when she felt she couldn't take another step, she realized Welton had picked her up. She must have dozed off in his arms for the next thing she knew she was being placed on the seat of the car.

"There. Now, before you know it, we'll have you in bed. Do you feel any better?" asked Jo.

"A little," was the brief reply. Jo saw that her face looked pinched and there were tiny lines of pain around her mouth.

When they returned Jo ran ahead to the camp site to get some blankets and to get Dick to help carry her sister. The anxious look on her face alarmed both Mavis and Dick when they saw her come running across the clearing.

"What's the matter? What's happened? Tell us, quickly!" Mavis rushed to her.

"It's Pat. She fell and hurt her knee. She can't walk." The staccato sentences tumbled out of Jo's mouth in rapid succession.

"Oh, dear! Why didn't Welty take her right to a doctor?" Mavis wrung her hands despairingly.

"Oh, don't be too alarmed, Mavis darling. I didn't mean to frighten you. I don't think Welty believes she's badly hurt. It's just a nasty bruise and the walk back to the car was so long. I'll get some blankets and Dick, if you'll come back with me, we can make a stretcher to carry her on."

"I'll get the blankets," Dick offered and ran to one of the tents. In a moment he was back. "There's no need for you to come with me, Jo, you look all tuckered out. Stay here and rest." He put his arm around her shoulders and squeezed her reassuringly. Then he turned and smiled at Mavis and gave her a mock salute. "I'll be back in a jiffy with her majesty."

His clowning eased the tension of the moment. When he had disappeared among the trees, Mavis picked up a pan and carried it over to the stream, saying to Jo, "If we put this in the water now it will be cold by the time they return with Patty. We haven't any ice, but the cold water will do just as well. It will help if the pan is cold, too."

By the time Pat had been carried back to the tent she was almost her old self again. The knee bothered her only a little, although little stabs of pain shot through her head now and then.

"I was careless and didn't see a tree coming toward me," she explained as Mavis plied her with questions. "I just forgot to duck. I'm all right, really."

Mavis insisted that she must lie down and, in spite of her protests, Jo and Mavis took turns keeping cool cloths on her head and knee. By nightfall the swellings had been reduced considerably.

Welton and Mavis sat before the campfire after the others had gone to bed that evening. "I think we had better return home, my dear. Patty won't be able to stand very well on that leg for a few days and it won't be much fun for her to stay here." Welton paused and drew reflectively on his pipe.

"I think you're right," Mavis returned. "I'd feel better if Dr. Gordon took a look at her knee, too."

"Well, the others will be disappointed, but I think that's the best thing to do." Welton yawned. "I'm sleepy. I think I'll turn in. Coming?"

"In a minute," Mavis answered.

She sat a few minutes longer, staring into the dying fire and listening to the night sounds. Bullfrogs croaked rhythmically and crickets chirped a dissonant accompaniment. A slim form moved quietly and sat down next to her. It was Jo.

"I couldn't sleep and when I saw your bed was empty, I thought I'd find you here."

"Is Pat asleep?" asked Mavis in a soft voice.

"Yes," Jo yawned. "She fell asleep right after supper and hasn't moved since."

"We're going home tomorrow. Welton thinks it would be best. You don't care, do you?"

"Gosh, no! I didn't want to say anything, but I thought we ought to. It's a shame our camping trip has to end this way, though, it was just perfect until today." A flame shot up momentarily and Mavis saw Jo turn impulsively toward her. "Honestly, Mavis, you and Welty do so much for us! Really, I think you're just wonderful. You know, I have a confession to make to you. Do you remember when, after we finally found Welty, we were so happy because he seemed to like us and to belong to us? Then, we felt just awful when you told us that you were going to be married because we thought you wouldn't want us, too. But you did—a-and—well, you're just swell, that's all."

"Yes," Mavis murmured softly, taking both of Jo's hands in her own, "I remember that day very well. I could read your mind, but, honey, didn't you know that we just wouldn't have planned it any other way? And you the sensible twin!"

"I 'spose so, but I'm not sensible all the time."

"You don't have to be," Mavis said tenderly, "and I think you're just right the way you are."

Jo and Mavis were both quiet for a moment, each thinking her own thoughts. Then Jo yawned and said, "I guess if I'm as sensible as everyone says I am, I should go to bed. We'll be getting up early, won't we?"

"Yes, we will. I'll come with you."

Everyone felt that the trip home the next day took much longer than it should. Actually, however, Welton had taken several shortcuts. They stopped at Dick's house only long enough to unload his luggage and then sped on home. Dick promised to come over the next day and see how Patty was.

Yamoto was surprised to see them and was greatly concerned over Pat's mishap. He went into her room first and made the bed ready so that she could rest immediately. Then he went out and started to unload the car with the help of the rest of the family.

Jo and Mavis had just come into the living

room when Patty rushed out of the bedroom as fast as she could with her lame knee. She looked terribly upset and excited.

"It's gone! Oh! Oh!"

Jo dropped her suitcase in alarm. "What is, Pat? What's gone?"

"The little drummer! I went to wind the music box and saw that the little figure with the snare drum wasn't there. I've hunted all over the room for it, but it's gone, I tell you. It's gone!"

7 Two Clues

"GONE?" Jo couldn't believe it. She dashed past
Pat, who was now weeping on Mavis's shoulder,
and looked herself. She picked up the music box
and looked under it and all around it where it
had stood on their chest of drawers. Then she
examined the chest itself, thinking it might possibly have been knocked into one of the drawers
when Yamoto was cleaning. After a thorough
search she returned to the living room, looking
sorrowful.

131

Patty had composed herself by this time and was now telling of the loss to Welton and Yamoto.

"Did you leave the house at all while we were gone, Yamoto?" she asked. She was lying on the couch, looking up at him.

And Yamoto remembered the day when he and Lucky went into the woods to chop wood. He told how he had thought someone was prowling about the house, but that he had made a thorough search of the house and found nothing. He had not noticed the music box at all, he said.

"I'm going outside and see if I can't find something there," Jo said firmly. "What day did you say this walk of yours was, Yamoto?"

"Thluhsday, Mlissy Jo."

"Hmmm," Jo murmured as she thought hard. "It rained where we were that day. Has it rained here?" She looked up at Yamoto inquiringly.

"Last evening lain some."

"Then the ground should have been soft enough for whoever it was to have left footprints. That might help."

She went out through the dining room and kitchen to the back door. Once outside, she went to the spot under their bedroom window. There she found many footprints close to the wall of the house—a place where no one would have occasion to walk unless he were trying to open the window.

Jo stood looking at the footprints and decided they were about the size and shape of a man's shoe. But there was something different about them, she couldn't decide just what it was.

Yamoto approached her and said he had remembered something else that he had forgotten to tell her before. "When I put wood away, Lucky act funny. Maybe someone hide in shed."

"We ought to look there, too, Yamoto, in that case. But look at these footprints. Do they look—well—sort of strange to you?"

"A man's shoe," said Yamoto, examining the footprints. "Eulopean shoe, I think. Heels difflent Amelican ones." Yamoto was visibly excited.

"Well, all we have to do is find someone who wears European shoes. That won't be very easy, I'm afraid." Jo looked at the window frame and at the shrubbery which grew close to the house to see if there was anything else that might be helpful to them. "The only trouble is," she said when she found nothing, "whoever took the drummer surely isn't waiting around for us to discover him. He could be miles away from here by now."

"You're right, my dear," came Welton's voice behind her. He, too, had come to examine the ground. "I've been checking over things in my study and everything seems to be in order there. I don't believe this person, whoever he is, took anything else."

"That's something to be thankful for, Welty. Golly, it is fortunate that none of your valuable fossils were taken!"

"Yes, yes, you're quite right. Now, what have you found here?"

Jo pointed out the footprints and told him Yamoto's theory. Welton thought it was a plausible one, but not of too much value. The three went to the tool shed next to inspect it. The ground was quite churned up at the entrance and it was impossible to separate any one footprint from another. A search in the surrounding area was equally unrewarding. Sadly Jo returned to the house.

Patty was lying propped up in her bed when Jo returned and reported to her the scant information they had found.

"I've been lying here thinking, Jo, and do you know what puzzles me the most?" Jo shook her head. "Why did he, whoever he is, take only that one figure? Why didn't he take the whole music box?"

"I hadn't thought of that, Patty. But now that you mention it, it is peculiar. And why did he only take that when Welty's got so many things in his study that are much more valuable?"

"Somehow he must have known it was here, Jo. Have we talked about our music box in the village where a stranger might have heard us?"

Jo wrinkled her brow in concentration. "Not that I can remember. Everyone we might have described it to was here at our birthday party, the night that Mavis gave it to us."

"Gosh! Remember the day Elaine was here and we played it for her? It was broken, wasn't it?"

"Do you suppose she might have mentioned it to someone, then? I mean, later after she left our house." Pat's thinking was paralleling Jo's.

"We'll ask her tomorrow," Jo decided. The girls were silent while they tried to think of other possible means of reaching a solution to the theft. It was, indeed, a puzzling occurrence.

That afternoon Dr. Gordon came to look at Pat's knee and pronounced it a bad bruise, but nothing more serious than that. He told Mavis to keep Pat from putting her weight on the leg for a few days longer. Then, he said, he would come back to see her again. If the swelling was not reduced at that time he would be able to tell if further treatment would be necessary.

The days dragged for Patty for she was used to being active. Time hung heavy on her hands and even though Jo kept her company much of the time, she longed to be out of bed. When Dr. Gordon visited her the second time her knee was its normal size and only slightly discolored. She was delighted when he said she might get up.

A night or so later Patty woke up suddenly. She did not know how late it was, but she knew that she had been asleep. "Is that you, Jo?" she called out. No answer.

She turned toward Jo's bed and the hump in

the middle of it told her that Jo was still beside her. She hesitated, panic-stricken, wondering whether to wake Jo or to lie silently watching. A stream of moonlight at that moment froze her and a scream of terror died on her lips. She was sure she was not imagining what she saw—a figure running away from their window!

Frantically she jumped out of bed and ran to the window. Which way was the figure running? Toward their woods! Patty slowly returned to her bed, her heart beating rapidly, knowing that it would be useless to give chase in the woods during the blackness of night. She resolved not to waken Jo after all, since there seemed nothing to do anyway. She listened and noticed that Jo was still peacefully asleep, breathing regularly.

Patty lay down again but she slept only fitfully during the remainder of the night. Once she heard Lucky growl in the back hall where he slept. It startled her again, but she decided he was only growling in his sleep.

At last the sky grew lighter with the approach of dawn and Patty dozed. She woke again about six o'clock, arose and dressed quietly in order not to disturb her sleeping twin. She softly opened their bedroom door, stepped quietly down the hall, opened the front door and slipped out.

Swiftly she walked to the rear of the house straight for the bedroom window. There she found what she needed to confirm her belief that she had not dreamt what she had heard the night before. "More footprints!" she breathed quietly to herself. "And they are strange-looking ones, moreover." She remembered what Jo had told her about the previous set she had found in the same spot.

Looking around carefully for more prints her eye lit upon a few shreds of cloth which clung to one of the shrubs. Carefully she untangled it from the clinging twigs. As she held it in her hand she noted that it seemed to be a heavy dark material of some sort, the kind from which a coat or a suit might be made. At this she sucked in her breath in wonderment. She turned and walked back toward the front of the house.

Jo found her half an hour later sitting on the steps of the front porch deep in thought.

"My! You're up early this morning, sis. How come?" Jo said as she pushed open the screen door. She came and stood behind her sister. "Been for a walk someplace? Your shoes are all wet."

Patty turned and looked at Jo in silence. At last she said, "Yes. Sit down while I tell you." Then she related the events of the previous night and that morning. She concluded the speech by showing Jo the piece of cloth she had found.

"Sa-ay," Jo exclaimed, as she turned the fragment over and over in her hands. "That's something, all right. I don't know what it means, but it's something."

"It tells us one encouraging thing, Jo, and that is just this. Whoever it is must be still in the neighborhood. We still have a chance to catch him. And that's something we weren't sure about before."

"At the same time, though," Jo said with a shiver, "it means that he must not have gotten everything he wanted. Else why would he come back again?"

"You're right. I hadn't thought of it that way."

Behind them Lucky whined at the screen door to be let out. Pat got up and opened it for him. He greeted her with a joyous bark of welcome. Then he ran down the steps and faced the girls as if to say, "Come on, let's play a bit. It's a wonderful morning!"

"Come here, Lucky," called Jo. She held out her hand. The dog came running, then he stopped and sniffed at the piece of cloth she still unconsciously held in her fingers. She looked down and had a sudden idea.

"Come on, Patty, let's try something with Lucky. Maybe he can help us find the thief. See how he's sniffing at this piece of material? Perhaps he's part bloodhound."

"Oh, Jo! That sounds like a crazy idea to me!"

"Well, what harm will it do? None, I tell you, and it may even do some good." Jo stood up and waved the cloth under Lucky's nose. "Go get 'em, boy, go get 'em," she repeated.

Thinking this was some new kind of game they were playing, Lucky raced around and around the yard in circles.

"You see, Jo, what did I tell you? He's just playing." Pat looked smug. She tossed her head and started for the door.

"Wait, Patty, maybe he's trying to get the scent. There! Now he's going around the house. After him!"

Still unconvinced, Patty rather half-heartedly followed her sister who ran after Lucky. Behind the house Lucky led them in the direction of the tool shed. Jo looked at her twin defiantly. "Who says our dog isn't smart? He knows what I wanted him to do."

The chase continued. At last Lucky stopped and began to dig furiously under the hedge that lined their yard. Jo was beside herself with excitement as she watched him. Suddenly he stopped digging and began tugging at something. When he had it in his mouth, he growled and turned around to offer his prize to Jo.

Patty started to laugh, pointing her finger at the bone in Lucky's mouth. "Some bloodhound you have there, Jo." So saying, she scooped up the dog, bone and all, and hugged him, still shaking with laughter.

Jo managed to smile ruefully and said rather lamely, "Well, it was just an idea. I didn't really think it would work."

"Let's forget about it for now and concentrate on finding breakfast. I'm hungry," Patty suggested. She turned and ran back to the kitchen door.

After breakfast that morning Patty and Jo related the latest news they had to Mavis and Welton. Mavis was frankly worried at the description of the new developments and expressed her worry aloud.

"Do you think it's safe, Welton? Perhaps this man is dangerous."

"I don't know what to think, now." Welton puffed reflectively on his pipe. "I feel this is getting to be a very serious matter. As you say, we have no idea what this man is like, so I think it would be advisable, Patty and Jo, if you do not roam about alone, particularly after dark."

"Okay, Welty," said Jo, a little disappointed that they could not track this man down by themselves. "We'll be careful."

"Do you suppose he might be hiding in the woods?" suggested Mavis, remembering that one dangerous man had been found there by the twins. "You say you saw him running in that direction, Patty."

"Possibly, possibly," answered Welton. "Yamoto and I will investigate them. No, girls, I won't let you come with us," he said as he saw their faces light up at the prospect of adventure. "It may be a dangerous mission, if we spot this man."

"Oh, please, Welty," Jo exclaimed. "We promise to do anything you say, if only you'll let us go along."

"Yes, Welty," Patty chimed in. "We'll keep out of the way. Besides, with you and Yamoto nothing could possibly happen to us." She attempted to flatter him into relenting.

Welton turned in desperation to his wife. "What do you say, my dear?"

She laughed shortly. "Oh, take them. They'll only be a handful here if you don't."

Patty and Jo kissed her and danced about excitedly. "When do we start?" Jo asked impatiently. "Let's go right now!"

"I suppose it would be best to go now," Welton agreed, smiling at the girls' enthusiasm. "If you'll go tell Yamoto to join us, we can be on our way. You won't be nervous here alone, Mavis?"

"No, no. Just leave Lucky here with me," she answered.

They decided that the hunters' shacks were the most likely places to look first. There were four of them scattered about the woods and they were unused at this time of the year. It would be easy for someone to live in one without anyone knowing about it.

Welton cautioned the girls to stay close beside him as they walked along toward the first shack. When they neared the small structure he told Patty and Jo to stay where they were while he and Yamoto went inside.

"If you see anyone or hear anything, signal to us with a whistle," he instructed them.

The girls obeyed and waited as they were told. They watched Yamoto and Welton approach the shack, carefully peering ahead in order to see into the interior. If someone were watching them, they would be prepared for him. Assured that everything was safe, they cautiously opened the door and stepped inside, leaving the door open for escape if needed.

In a few moments they stepped out again, satisfied that this one, at least, had been undisturbed. The dusty floor would have told them at once if the place were being used. Festoons of cobwebs hung from the ceiling in undisturbed peace. Only a midget could have walked beneath them without disturbing them.

The party tramped on through the woods and followed the same procedure at each of the remaining three shacks. They found nothing in any of them.

"It eases my mind a great deal to know this," Welton stated as they reported their trip to Mavis on their return. "I'm satisfied that our woods were merely a means of escape and not a refuge."

The twins were secretly disappointed that no excitement had presented itself in the woods, but they did not give voice to their opinions. Mavis sighed with relief at the news.

That afternoon Patty and Jo accompanied Yamoto into the village to meet Mrs. Gruber who was returning from her short holiday. She, of course, was unaware of the fact that the Duers had cut short their fishing trip and Mavis had said there was no reason to call her back earlier.

Yamoto had allowed ample time in which to reach the village before the bus was due and so they had a short wait before it arrived. The twins were idly watching the crowd of people who were also awaiting the bus when suddenly Pat reached out and twitched Jo's sleeve.

"Look over there, Jo!" she said in an excited whisper. "I do believe the coat that man is wearing has a rip in one sleeve! Do you suppose . . ."

"It's the same color!" Jo agreed and edged nearer to the man.

"He's walking away," noted Patty. "Let's follow him. Come on, Jo!"

Off she went with Jo close behind her. The man was walking quickly down the street. He turned his head once, looking back over his shoulder. When this happened, Patty and Jo stopped quickly and pretended to be looking in one of the shop windows. The glass pane mirrored the man's reflection and as soon as he started walking again, the watchful girls were once again in pursuit.

They had studied the man, hoping for a good look at his face, but unfortunately they were unable to see it clearly enough. His reflection had been only a blur because of the distance between him and the window.

Running a little in order to keep pace with the man's long, rapid strides, the twins observed his back in silence, but they both noticed that the jacket he wore was not an American one. They were sure that his shoes would be different, also! Their description of him afterwards included only the fact that he was quite tall and had rather narrow shoulders.

Suddenly a small boy dashed in front of them and Patty nearly tripped. In the few seconds it took her to recover her balance with Jo's help, the man disappeared. They had only looked away for a moment, but a moment had been enough.

"Oh, dear!" Jo mourned when they were forced to give up. "We nearly had him that time."

"Jo," exclaimed her sister in a hushed voice, "we've got to keep watch for him. We've just got to!"

"How? You know Welty won't let us out of his sight unless Yamoto's with us."

"I don't know yet. But we must think of a plan!"

8 *In Pursuit*

PATTY AND Jo walked back to the bus stop and
joined Yamoto, who had begun to wonder where
they were. A cloud of dust far down the street
heralded the approach of the bus. Soon it lurched
to a stop in front of them and Mrs. Gruber was
one of the first to alight, awkwardly pulling her
suitcase down the steps. Yamoto quickly took the
bag from her and she sighed.

"My land! Such a hot, dusty trip. I thought it
would never end," she complained. Her hat was

askew and her dress was rumpled. Her whole appearance made one think she was more discontented than usual.

Spying the twins she said, "Well, well, a welcoming party. You're back early, aren't you?"

Yamoto led the way to the spot where he had parked the car and Patty and Jo began to tell Mrs. Gruber all the things that had happened during the time she had been gone. They were turning into the driveway when the twins finished their story.

Mrs. Gruber looked glum. "The minute my back's turned, something awful happens," she said morosely. "You girls had better stay out of trouble now, that is, if you can. You just seem to attract excitement and mysterious goings-on. Oh, well, I suppose it's none of my affair," she ended grumblingly.

Patty checked an impulse to reply to her. She decided that anything she might say would merely aggravate the situation. Jo, too, wisely kept still.

Welton and Mavis came outside to greet Mrs. Gruber and after they had finished inquiring about her trip Welton turned to the girls and said, "Those strange footprints in the mud underneath your window frankly worry me. I don't like the idea of this fellow returning last night. Who knows? He may return again. Even though we made a thorough search of the woods this morning and found nothing, it does not mean that the man is not in this vicinity. Therefore, I've decided to call in a private detective to get to the bottom of this."

"Oh, gee, Welty, let us do the detectiving, please!" Jo pleaded.

"We solved a mystery once before. Remember, Welty?" Patty added to her sister's plea. She thought of how near they had come to catching a suspicious-looking man only that afternoon, but said nothing about it.

Their requests were in vain, however, for Welton shook his head decidedly. "This man may be dangerous or ruthless, or both. I can't risk your getting hurt tracking him down. No, it's all settled. I have already put a call through to a detective agency in Palmerdale. They are sending a man out here tomorrow."

Both girls looked crushed and Mavis, in spite

of the fact that she shared Welton's anxiety in the matter, felt sympathetic toward the girls' desire for adventure. "I'm sure the detective will want to hear all about the clues you have found. Won't that be some compensation for not trying to solve it by yourselves? He'll need your help."

Patty and Jo were not comforted by this suggestion, although they were grateful to Mavis for her understanding.

"I suppose Welty's right," Jo conceded, "but I just know we could trap this man if we could find him."

"He's elusive, I'll grant you," Patty murmured.

"Well, now, the case will be in competent hands by tomorrow," Welton said. "The detective will know the best way to find this man for us. He's an expert in such matters."

Later that day when Patty and Jo were alone they decided not to show the detective the piece of cloth they had found until they were sure it would help him. And because they were not sure that the man they had chased that afternoon was the right one, they said nothing to anyone about that, either.

The night passed without another nocturnal visit, and early the next morning a short, gray-haired man in his early forties knocked on the door of Welton Duer's lodge. He introduced himself to Yamoto, who answered his knock, as Mr. Dunbar from the detective agency in Palmerdale.

Yamoto found Welton in his study with Mavis and the twins, and informed them of their visitor. The three joined the detective in the living room. Patty and Jo were somewhat disappointed in Mr. Dunbar. He did not behave in the way they imagined a private detective should. Instead of being alert and intense, he seemed rather casual and unemotional about his assignment. Both of the girls were sure he would not solve the mystery.

"I understand you've been bothered by a prowler recently," Mr. Dunbar began. He twirled his hat on his finger, as he sat before them.

"That is right," Welton answered. Then he proceeded to tell the man what had happened since Patty had discovered that the drummer was missing. From time to time Jo and Patty added other facts that Welton forgot to mention. Mr. Dunbar pulled a small notebook from his hip pocket and made short notations on some of the details of their story.

When Welton finished Mr. Dunbar closed his notebook and tapped its cover lightly with his fingers. Then he spoke. "We haven't much to work with, Mr. Duer, but we'll do our best with what we have. You say there were footprints. Are they still visible?"

"Yes. Come, I'll show them to you," Welton said and rose from his chair.

Patty and Jo followed the two men outside. They watched as Mr. Dunbar knelt down to examine the footprints closely. He pointed his finger at the heel of one of them.

"This looks as if a knife was used to cut the leather, but that doesn't mean much. Hmm, well, I'll make a note of it, anyway. Now, I think I will explore a bit by myself and see if I can find anything else of interest. There's no need for you to inconvenience yourselves any longer. If I have any more questions to ask you, I'll come back. Thank you for the information you have given me, scant as it is."

His curt manner prevented Patty and Jo from accompanying him in his explorations, much as they wanted to.

"I don't think he's very interested in the case," Jo confided to Patty when they were alone. "Let's continue to watch for clues by ourselves."

"You're right, Jo, he didn't seem particularly concerned. Do you know what I think? I think he believes we imagined most of the things that happened and that the drummer is just lost and not stolen at all!"

"Well, that's all the more reason for our going ahead on our own," Jo agreed.

The following afternoon Patty and Jo met Dick, George and Elaine on the beach. Dick, of course, knew that the toy drummer was missing, but George and Elaine had not heard the story.

"And it was so maddening to lose that man right when we almost had him," Jo moaned. "If I ever see that little boy again, I—I don't know what I'll do," she finished lamely.

"However," George reasoned, "even if you had caught him, what good would that have been?

All he would need to have done was to tell you that you had the wrong guy. You can't prove it was he who took it. Why, you can't prove that anyone took it, really."

George's cold logic cast a new light on their problem. "I never thought of what we'd do," Pat put in. "We were so intent on catching him that we didn't think of a scheme."

Elaine rolled over on the beach towel and let the sun strike her back. She flicked the sand from the towel, then lay down again. Her words were muffled as she spoke without lifting her head. "You would have thought of something. Pay George no attention, Patty, he's one of those men who think women should be helpless creatures."

Patty laughed at her words which George failed to hear. "What did you say, sis?" George asked.

Elaine sat up. "I was only revealing a phase of your character that these girls should know about. I don't have to repeat it to you. You know it already." She grinned at him mischievously. "Seriously, though, can't we all do something? Organize a spy system? Do some scouting?

"You have nothing to go on," George repeated, shaking his head.

The group looked gloomy as they considered the truth of his statement. It was perfectly true, a missing toy drummer and a few shreds of cloth were hardly conclusive evidence.

"I still can't imagine what anyone would want with just part of that music box," Jo said, reviewing the facts once more. "Why not take the whole thing?"

"It sure doesn't make sense," Dick agreed. His face lit up as an idea came to him. Excitedly he said, "Say, why don't we look at those figures again? Perhaps we can find an answer to that question."

"I don't understand," Patty said, looking puzzled. "What good would that do?"

"I think I see what Dick means," Jo interrupted as Dick was about to explain himself. "If the figures are different in some way, I don't know exactly how, it would explain why he took one and not all of them. He surely had a reason for wanting only one of them."

"Let's go up to the house and look at them

right now," Patty urged, seeing a chance for new discovery.

They all scrambled up the cliff in great haste with Lucky barking at their heels. Once in the girls' room they immediately set about examining the figures. Jo picked up the flute player first. She turned it slowly over in her hand.

"I don't see anything strange about this one, do you?" she said. They all agreed as she picked up the accordion player.

"Before you look at that one, Jo," Patty suggested, "look at the bass drummer. Remember that the other one was a drummer, too."

"Wonderful idea, Patsy." Jo picked it up and tapped it with her finger. "Listen to this. Doesn't it sound hollow?"

Patty held her breath and nodded. She picked up the flute player again and tapped it. "This one isn't hollow."

"Wait!" Jo said excitedly. She pushed the bottom of the drum itself and before their eyes it slid off.

"Look inside!" Patty directed in an excited tone of voice.

All heads bent over as Jo turned the drum upside down and they peered in. They could see nothing.

Everyone except Pat looked disappointed at this. But she said in a trembling voice, "Don't you see? It means that the other drummer probably did have something inside of it. I think that's important, don't you?"

Jo's face brightened. "You're absolutely right, Patty. Of course that's the answer! Now there's something else I just thought of that's very puzzling. Why did the man return last night? What did he want?"

Dick spoke up then. He said, "Perhaps he hoped there might be something in this drummer. He certainly knew there were two of them if he knew there were any at all. It seems to me that this man knows a great deal more than we do about your music box."

"All of this thinking has made me dreadfully thirsty," Patty commented as Dick finished. "How about the rest of you? Would you like some nice cold lemonade?"

The others agreed with her suggestion and

they all went out to the shady porch, where Patty brought the cool drinks a few minutes later. They sat quietly, holding the icy glasses and watching the drops of moisture form on the surface. With the tip of her finger, Jo idly traced a design in the wetness.

It was George who broke the silence. "Not to change the subject, interesting though it is, but there is going to be a carnival in the village to-night. I saw the advertisement in the drugstore window this morning. Why don't we all go?"

"Carnivals are such fun!" Patty and Jo agreed simultaneously.

"I'll ask Welty and Mavis if we can go," Patty jumped up, again full of energy. She skipped into the house and found them both in Welton's study. Returning again to the porch she replied that she had secured their permission. "They say we have to be home early, though," she reported.

"I'll see if Mother will let me have the car and I can pick you up about eight, then," Dick offered.

The party that rolled through the countryside that evening was a gay one. They were all in a

party mood and sang songs as Dick expertly drove
the car toward the village. From a distance they
could see the gay colored lights that marked the
carnival, which was set up at the outskirts of the
town on the opposite side from Welton Duer's
home.

In the field across from the carnival grounds
were many parked cars. It was difficult to find
space, for many people from the surrounding area
had arrived ahead of them. Finally Dick found a
space and maneuvered the car into it. The party
piled out and started across the road toward the
carnival.

Once inside the entrance they found themselves in the midst of a carefree, joyous crowd,
all seeking, as they were, an evening of entertainment. They looked about them as they walked
and saw sideshows being advertised in loud
voices by the barkers. There was a tame animal
show, a strong man act, a group of aerial artists,
trapeze performers and jugglers. Off to one side
they saw a merry-go-round, a ferris wheel and a
roller coaster. Refreshment stands were set up at
frequent intervals, and hot dogs, hamburgers,

soft drinks, candy, popcorn and peanuts were being sold in unbelievable quantities.

George went off to one of these stands and came back with five bags of popcorn. He handed one to each of them, keeping one for himself, and they all munched as they walked along.

"Let's watch the trained animals," Patty suggested, when they came in front of the tent where a barker was calling loudly. "They're always fun. I hope they have a trained bear."

Everyone agreed and Dick went over to the window and purchased their tickets. Inside there were several rows of benches and a small stage, which was curtained at the moment, stood at the end. The group found seats together and waited eagerly for the curtain to be raised.

"I remember one act I saw once," giggled Elaine, "when one of those cute little dogs they had went the wrong way off stage and landed in somebody's lap. He was so small that the lady who caught him put him in her pocket and all you could see was his nose poking up from the top."

Just then the curtain rose and a series of acts

followed. Patty watched with delight when a bear lumbered through a simple dance, graceful in spite of his size. When it was over they emerged once more into the crowd outside.

"Where to, now?" Dick asked as they stood uncertainly outside the tent.

"Do you want to ride on the roller coaster?" asked Elaine, wanting to herself, but being polite.

"Sure," answered Jo for the rest of them. "Which way is it?"

"This way," said Dick, seizing her hand. "Come along."

There was quite a line of people waiting when they got to the roller coaster. There were only two cars of three seats each running, which did not accommodate many riders at once. At last it was their turn and they scrambled in as the car slowed before them. Jo, Dick and Patty landed in one seat together, with George and his sister behind them.

Just as the car began to move, Jo froze in her seat. Seeing this, Dick leaned over and said, "What's the matter? You look as if you had just seen a ghost."

Jo just looked at him, motioning him not to say anything more. Finally she found her voice and whispered, "Don't say a word, but I think that's our man right ahead of us! Ask Patty," she said this last in an urgent tone of voice.

Dick, in turn, whispered the information to Patty and she looked, turned and nodded to Jo. She, too, looked nervous.

The twins could hardly wait for the ride to end and as soon as the car slowed down they hopped out, each intent on following the stranger.

He was directly in front of Patty as they started down the steps. They were about halfway down when Jo noticed something drop from his pocket. She stopped abruptly so that Dick, who was just behind her, nearly fell over her. Down between the flat boards which made up the stairway went a little object. It dropped some fifteen feet below on the gravel. The jostle of the crowd behind her brought Jo back from her thoughts and she hurried down the steps.

As soon as she reached the bottom she ran to the spot where the object had dropped. She stooped to pick it up and there, just as she had hoped, lay the little wooden drummer!

Unfortunately the drum had been broken from the rest of the figure in its fall and lay a few feet away. Jo gathered up the two pieces and looked around for her friends. Where were they? Suddenly she spied them and went running in their direction.

"Where's Patty?" she asked breathlessly as she reached the group and saw that Patty was not with them.

They looked at each other blankly and then realized Patty was not there.

"I'll bet I know!" exclaimed Jo. "She's gone off in pursuit of that man. Oh, dear! Help me somebody! We've just got to find her!" Jo's voice showed that she was very close to tears.

"We'll separate," George said in a quiet voice that reassured Jo quickly. "Elaine and I will go that way and you and Dick go in the opposite direction. We'll meet at the main gate."

Dick took Jo by the arm and guided her along the crowded path. "We'll find her, Jo. She didn't have too fast a start on us."

"B-but anything m-might happen to her," Jo

stuttered. She was crying but she didn't care. "That man might h-have a g-gun."

"We'll just pray that he doesn't," Dick said grimly. This was one time when he couldn't think of something to say that might cheer her up. His eyes swiftly searched the crowd ahead for a glimpse of Patty.

Jo held on to Dick's hand tightly. "I know he's the one now, look," she said.

Dick hardly looked at the little drummer which she held clutched in her other hand. "Good," he said briefly. Actually, however, he was even more concerned and anxious to find Patty now that they were sure.

Meanwhile, far ahead of them walked Patty intent on the figure of a man who walked swiftly in and out of the crowd. He did not pause to examine any of the booths which lined the path. He seemed merely intent upon leaving the carnival. Patty was almost out of breath when the crowd thinned out before her and she realized that there was no one between her and the man.

She had almost overtaken him when, suddenly, he whirled. "See here, young lady," growled the pursued, "what do you want? I've known you were following me ever since I left that, what do you Americans call it, that roller coaster."

Patty gasped. Not only because she had been taken unawares, but also because she saw the stranger clearly for the first time.

9 *The Case Is Solved*

"ANSWER MY question," commanded the stranger, his dark eyes ablaze.

Patty continued to stare at him. He was a boy not much older than herself, rather tall, and quite handsome even in anger. He was the same boy she and Jo had discussed that day in Lampson when they had gone to the market! His jacket was the same as the one worn by the stranger she and Jo had followed in the village. Putting two and two together, the excited girl realized that the stranger in Lampson and the man she and Jo had seen when they went with Yamoto to meet Mrs. Gruber were one and the same person! Perhaps she was right when she had first mentioned to Jo on the market day so long ago that the stranger walking hurriedly in the opposite direction was a spy on some sort of secret mission. If this were true, what should she do now?

"Well," said the boy, becoming a little uncertain of himself as Patty remained silent, "what do you have to say for yourself?"

"Why did you take it," Patty asked, a little sadly.

"Take what? I don't know what you're talking about?" The boy's dark eyebrows met in a frown as he assumed his previous attitude of bluster.

"You know perfectly well what I mean," returned Patty, now a little angry herself. "Why did you want to spoil our music box?"

The boy stepped back a few paces. He was completely surprised. He had not expected this mere girl to confront him with that. He had imagined Mrs. Duer to be an older woman.

Just then Jo and Dick rushed up. Dick seized

the boy roughly, immediately sizing him up and feeling confident that he could handle him if he started getting violent.

"Patty, darling, are you all right?" breathlessly asked Jo. She embraced her twin rather hysterically.

"Yes, yes, of course," Patty said and returned her sister's embrace. "Remember him?" she asked, whispering in Jo's ear.

Jo stood back and surveyed the young man. Turning to Pat in astonishment, she said, "He's the boy we saw in Lampson, isn't he?"

"That's what I thought, too."

"Has he admitted anything yet?" Jo asked.

"He was about to when you and Dick came up."

"Then maybe this will do the trick." Jo opened her hand and extended the toy drummer toward the boy. "You dropped this, I believe?"

The boy stopped struggling with Dick and dropped his hands to his sides as he eyed the figure. "Very well," he said in a dull voice, "I surrender."

Patty felt a little compassionate for him, then, he looked so beaten. She wondered how someone like that could bring himself to take something that didn't belong to him. "It just doesn't add up, somehow," she thought to herself.

"I'll tell you the whole story, but it's a long one. Do you suppose we could sit down somewhere?" The boy appealed to them not only with his words, but with his eyes.

There was a refreshment stand not far away that held two small tables in it. Dick led the group toward it in silence. Jo and Patty had never seen him look so stern. They sat down at one of the tables and the boy nervously began his story.

"My name is Leonardo Amerigo," he began, nervously lacing and unlacing the fingers of his hands together.

"I'm Patty Faraday and this is my sister, Jo, and this is Dick Prentiss," Patty said, wanting somehow to make this distasteful business a little more friendly.

Jo said hello and Dick nodded curtly. He saw no reason for turning this thing into a regular tea party.

"Ah," continued Leonardo, "I was puzzled about you at first." This was addressed to Patty.

"I thought you were Mrs. Duer, but I did not understand how one so young . . ."

"Let's stick to the point," Dick muttered sternly.

"Excuse me, where was I? Ah, I know, I had only told you my name. I come here from my home in Italy where I live with my father. He is a poor shopkeeper there. However, once we had enough money saved for me to come to your country to go to school. You see, long ago Papa wanted to come here himself, but he never managed it. His reasons were simple enough, his name—my name, too—is the same as the Italian name for your country." He turned to Dick beside him and said, "My telling you my name has some importance now, hasn't it?"

"Some."

Leonardo turned back to the girls. "Since my father could not come here, he wanted very much for me to come instead and it was all planned out when I was a little boy. At that time, an uncle of mine, my father's brother, died and left his estate to me. He was quite rich—at least—he seemed quite rich to us. His estate consisted of a number of American securities and his house, that is all."

Leonardo shifted in his seat. "The American securities were to pay for my education in your country. Then the war came along and first my uncle's house was confiscated. My father was so worried that they might take the securities, also, that he had a film made of them which reduced them in size."

"Do you mean they were microfilmed?" Jo asked.

"Is that what you call it? I do not know the word, but it is perhaps the same thing. Afterward Papa burned the securities and hid the mi—microfilm in the music box. You see, my father owns the shop where Mrs. Duer bought the music box she now has. May I ask you a question? Are you friends of hers, is that it?"

Patty quickly explained the relationship.

"I see," he replied. "Papa is getting old now and doesn't remember things quite so well as he used to. He sold the music box, not realizing at the time what was hidden inside of it. It was not until this year, when I prepared to come to this country, that he thought of them again. He was in despair when he remembered selling the box, but he had a plan. You see, he remembered that a woman had bought the music box the year following the war. It was not hard to check his register for names of tourists for that year, because there were not many tourists then. He also remembered that the woman was an American, for he had chatted with her about your country. He is anxious to know all he can about it even now.

"We scraped together enough money for my passage and it was Papa's plan that I visit all the people on his list. There were not many names, only four or five, so it did not seem a difficult task. But I did not have very much money and I cannot work here without a permit. I have only permission to study here and I have passed my examinations at one of your universities. Everything is in order except the money. Well, I walked and I—what do you call it with the thumb—hitchhiked from one city to another until I had visited all of the people on my list except one. She, this Mrs. Duer, was hard to find. She had, of course, married since and moved—but you know all that.

"The next part of my story is hard to put into

words. How can I explain to you how very much this means to me, even more to my father? It would have been a fulfillment of a dream for him. How can I explain my desperation when I found no one was there when I came? How can I explain that I lost all reason when, after months of searching, I saw my, pardon me, *your* music box? As I say, it is hard to tell you this. Can you understand my vague phrases?" He stopped and looked pleadingly at Patty.

"I—I think I know what you mean," she answered in a soft voice.

"Humph. He's pleading temporary insanity, that's what he's doing," Dick said shortly.

"Oh, Dick, how can you be so unfeeling!" Jo snapped. His brusque manner was becoming annoying to her and it was so unlike him to be unfriendly.

"I may be unfeeling, but you, honey, are acting very gullible," Dick snapped back.

"What do you mean by that, may I ask?" Jo drew herself up.

"May I speak frankly?" Dick inquired. Jo nodded coldly. "Well, then, here sits this fellow

handing us a lot of sentimental phrases and ask-
ing us to understand how he feels and what has
he got to lose? Nothing, I'll answer it for you. He
has what he came for and now he says he's sorry
that he took it underhandedly."

"Oh, you misunderstand," Leonardo said in a
quiet voice. "I do not have the microfilm, if that
is what you mean. Someone evidently found their
hiding place before I did. I have looked, but they
are not there. It is most likely that my father's
memory played tricks on him; that he does not
remember giving them up to the authorities. As
I stated at the beginning I surrender to you. Do
what you like, call the police if you wish."

"Oh, we couldn't do that!" Patty exclaimed.

"Well, no, I—I, gee, I don't know," Dick said
in a perplexed voice. "It was wrong of you to
enter the house without permission."

"You're right," Leonardo said humbly.

"Let's leave it up to Welty, then," Jo suggested,
"it's his house, you know."

"That's the best plan," Patty agreed. "And besides, I have an idea we may still find that
microfilm!"

"Do you mean it?" Leonardo's eyes grew large.

"I can't promise anything yet. But, come along, let's go home."

"Wait, we've forgotten about George and Elaine," reminded Dick. "They said they'd wait for us at the main entrance."

The party got up from the table in the small refreshment stand and left. They headed back toward the main gate and there they found George and Elaine waiting anxiously. They eyed Leonardo as their friends approached.

"Are you all right, Patty?" murmured Elaine, as Patty drew up beside her.

"Yes. It's a long story, but we'll tell you all about it in just a minute." Patty then introduced Leonardo to her two friends.

"Please," interrupted Leonardo, as Patty told his name to the Andersons, "in America I have learned that you are very fond of the shortened first name. Please call me Leo, it seems friendlier."

"Oh," Jo laughed, "you mean your nickname."

"That is it. I had forgotten the exact word."

As they drove home, Jo and Patty, with a little help from Leo, as they now called him, brought George and Elaine up to date on the events of the evening. They, too, were inclined to be critical at first, then sympathetic, as the story unfolded. Since it was getting late, the Andersons reluctantly asked Dick to drop them at their home, much as they would have liked to go back to the Duers and hear the outcome. But, they decided, they would wait to hear from Patty and Jo the next day, and the twins promised to call them.

After they had left George and Elaine, Leo asked the girls to tell him how they had discovered him.

"Those two are regular detectives," explained Dick, first of all.

"We found footprints near the window first," Patty began. "Then you tore your coat on the shrubbery the second time you came. That's when we knew for sure that the drummer wasn't just lost. And we knew you were still somewhere in the vicinity. This brings up something else, why did you come back that night? You scared me, let me tell you."

"Ah, you see, my conscience was bothering me then, especially since I had not found the microfilm. I felt badly that I had taken the figure, although at first I reasoned that it was really mine.

So I decided to put it back, but I did not think you would be home. So it was you who called out?"

"Yes. Then I looked out of the window and saw you running away."

Patty and Jo found that Mavis and Welton were still up when they brought Leo into the house. The twins were quite excited and the story of the discovery was quite jumbled at first.

"We found it and it was really his," Patty burst out when they entered the living room.

"Yes," affirmed Jo, "and please say he can stay here."

"What? Who? What in the world are you two imps talking about. Remember your manners and introduce this young man properly." Welton looked puzzled, stern and amused at the same time.

"Oh, I'm sorry, Welty," Pat apologized. "This is Leonardo Amerigo and his father owns the shop in Italy. Leo, this is our family, Mr. and Mrs. Duer."

"How do you do," Leo shook hands with each of them.

"We're pleased to meet you, young man,"

Welton said. "Now, Patty my girl, you're still not making any sense. What shop do you mean? Sit down, now, all of you, and organize your thoughts. Begin at the beginning."

Gradually, with some degree of coherence, the whole story was told for the third time that evening. When Leo explained that his father was a shopkeeper in Italy, Mavis excitedly interrupted his story. "Of course! I knew you seemed familiar to me. Why, I remember your father well and you resemble him a great deal. Now that I think of it, your father seemed reluctant to sell the music box, although he did not say why at the time. I merely thought he was fond of it for sentimental reasons, perhaps."

"Naturally you could not know the real reason," Leo agreed. He then finished his story and again he apologized profusely for taking and then breaking the toy drummer.

"I lost my head, sir, when I saw the music box through the window. Before I knew it there I was in that room, taking the figure. At the sound of footsteps I became frightened and ran away. It wasn't until later that I realized I had taken something that didn't rightfully belong to me. I tried later to put it back, thinking it might not have been missed, but the night I returned here I heard someone call out, Patty tells me it was she, so I didn't do it."

"So then everything has turned out for the best, has it?" Welton questioned him. He surveyed the young man as if he were an attorney in a courtroom.

"Oh, no, sir, I didn't mean it that way at all," Leo paused and ran his thin fingers nervously through his hair. "I understand that there is no excuse for what I have done. I only wanted to explain to you that I never did such a thing before nor did I plan to do this. I know what your duty is, however, and I—I'm—what is the phrase your gangsters use?—turning oneself in, I believe —that's all." His shoulders sagged as if he had just been relieved of a heavy burden. He put his elbows on his knees, chin in hand, and stared at the floor.

"Oh, Welty," Patty and Jo chorused in shocked tones, "don't let him do that!"

"Let me see," Welton said slowly, weighing his decision. "I see no reason to do that. The mystery has been solved and the girls have their wooden figure back, damaged though it is. While it is unfortunate that this whole thing happened at all, I believe you have suffered enough in your struggle with your conscience and I don't imagine you'll be tempted to do such a thing again."

"Oh, thank you, sir. You are much too kind and generous with me." Leo jumped to his feet, checked an impulse to embrace Welton and then shook his hand vigorously. "But you won't regret your decision, Mr. Duer, I swear it. And I'll fix the drummer, too, so like an expert that the break will never show."

Patty and Jo looked at each other happily. They whispered something to each other and tip-toed out of the room. An atmosphere of friendliness was now restored in the Duers' living room as Dick grinned genially and offered his hand to Leo as a friend.

"Forgive me for misjudging you earlier. Perhaps you can understand my skepticism at first. But if Welton says you're okay, then I say you are, too."

Leo returned his handshake firmly. At that

moment Patty and Jo reappeared bringing the music box with them. They set it down on the coffee table where everyone could see it.

"Now, let's look at the little drummer again," Jo turned to Dick. "Remember we examined it before? Well, Patty has an idea. You do it, Patty."

Patty took the little drummer out of the slot and carefully pushed the bottom of the drum toward one side. Again the bottom slid off as it had for Jo. Then Patty reached in and felt all around the sides.

"I think," she said, "there's something all rolled up inside here."

Leo could scarcely contain his feelings. He watched the girl, holding his breath. With the tip of her fingernail she managed to catch the corner of whatever it was. Then slowly she coaxed it from the container. It seemed an interminable length of time to Leo before the papers were in his hands. But at last Patty drew them out of the drum and placed them in Leo's shaking fingers.

"Ah, these are the ones, these are the ones," he repeated, half talking to himself. He handed them to Welton, so that he could verify them. They were tied together with a little piece of string and around them was a faded piece of paper bearing Leonardo's name in a cramped handwriting.

"Well, my boy," Welton said at last, handing them back to him, "you should consider yourself very fortunate. Yes, very fortunate, indeed."

"And to think how carelessly I treated the music box sometimes," Mavis said, shaking her head in wonderment.

"At this moment," Leo faltered, holding the papers dramatically before him, "I feel happier than I have felt ever all my life!"

10 Summer Farewell

EVERYONE IN the room was touched by Leo's
display of emotions. They thought of how glad
they were that Leo had what he had needed and
they reflected on their own good fortunes, varied
as they were. It was quiet in the room following Leo's speech until he, himself, broke the
silence.

"I must go now. It is very late and you will
want to retire, I am sure. I will say no more, only

simply thank you. My father has told me many times that I talk too much and do too little. This time I will show you. I will do something, also. I do not know what it will be yet. One thing I know I can do. That is, I will fix the little drummer. May I take it with me, Patty and Jo?"

"Of course, if you wish," Jo said, looking at her twin for approval. She picked up the drummer from the table and handed it to him. Leo wrapped the pieces in his handkerchief and stuffed the bundle into his pocket.

"Can I drop you off anywhere, Leo?" Dick asked, as he fumbled in his pocket for his keys.

"There is no need. I live in the village. It is not far and I can walk it easily." He laughed then, a little embarrassed, as he thought of his several trips over the same road on foot.

The others laughed self-consciously, too. Mavis gracefully filled the breach by saying, "You must come back soon. Plan to come for dinner Tuesday."

"I will be honored and pleased," Leo replied, bowing a little. "And now, goodnight."

When they had closed the door, Jo and Patty

flung themselves at Mavis and Welton in sheer delight. They were so pleased that everything had turned out so well.

"I adore you," Patty told Welton impulsively. "You did just what I hoped you'd do."

"Well, darling, I think he deserved considerate treatment, don't you?" Welton replied.

"Oh, of course, I do!" Patty said. She wandered around the room aimlessly. "He talks so nice. It's beautiful, almost. I've never known anyone who spoke the way he does."

"I'll call the detective agency first thing tomorrow morning," Welton resolved. "The detective wasn't as alert as you two were, I'm afraid."

"Leo's certainly well-mannered," Mavis commented.

"Yes. Did you see how he bowed to you when you asked him to dinner?"

"Look out," Jo said, looking mischievous. "I think Patty's about to go into a swoon."

Patty glared at her sister, but Jo looked so comical as she held her head far back with her arms stretched out that Patty had to laugh in spite of herself.

"Oh, dear," she laughed, "if I thought I was

going to look like that, I don't think I'd try it."

"Well, you would," Jo said. "I'll tell you something maybe you don't know. We're twins."

"No! Really?" Patty giggled.

"Yes, really," Jo laughed back.

"You two had better stop this nonsense," Mavis smiled. "What would anyone say if I suggested a cup of cocoa right now?"

"We'd love it," Jo and Patty said together.

The following Tuesday when Leo came for dinner he had lots of things to tell them. He had not seen them in the intervening period and he had been very busy arranging his affairs.

"First of all," he said, "I sent a cable to Papa telling him the good news. I received an answer already from him. He is overwhelmed with joy."

"I expect so," Patty answered.

"Then I wrote a letter to the college telling them that I was here and that I would arrive there the first of September. That is not very far away now."

"Where are you going to school, my boy?" Welton inquired.

"It is a small engineering college here in the

Midwest. Its name is Rogers College. Perhaps you've heard of it?"

"Heard of it? I should say I have, Leo!" Welton looked delighted.

"Dad and Welton both graduated from Rogers, Leo," Patty explained. "Gosh, isn't it a coincidence?"

"It proves that saying you have. It is, I believe, that it's a small world."

"That's right," Jo chimed in. "And it's very true, too. Gee, Welty, Rogers is quite near Colton College, where Patty and I are going. Some of the girls have told me that the Rogers boys and Colton girls often have joint dances and other affairs."

"Right you are, Jo. Well, you three shall be seeing something of each other, then, I expect." Welton looked very pleased.

"If you and Patty will permit me?" Leo said in his most polite manner.

Patty blushed prettily and merely said, "Of course."

Yamoto appeared to announce dinner, and Leo offered an arm to each girl as they went into the dining room.

The evening was a gay one in which the girls became better acquainted with Leo. He told them some amusing stories of his boyhood in Italy, and the twins had some adventures of their own to relate to him. Mavis reminisced with him of her visit to Europe and Welton recalled some interesting archeological expeditions he had made during his early career.

In the days that followed Leo found himself caught up in the whirl of fun and excitement that seemed to surround Patty and Jo wherever they went. Leo had none of the carefree gaiety which was a general characteristic shared by the twins' American friends. He was rather inclined to be serious and introspective. His gallantry of manner pleased equally adults and his contemporaries.

It was his very differences that drew Leo into the closely knit group, rather than setting him apart from them as one might expect. Mutual benefits were reaped; Leo took on some of the easy informality of Patty and Jo, and they, in turn, found themselves copying his tactful manner and poise.

There was a rush of activity as the summer drew to a close. Everyone seemed anxious to crowd as much as they could into each day, as though, almost, they thought summer would not come again. The season was climaxed by a street dance which was held annually in the village and which everyone, young and old, attended. For a week or more beforehand, it was the main subject of conversation.

Patty and Jo looked forward to it eagerly, as it was new to them, and the many descriptions which came to them from people on every side both intrigued and excited them. It was, they learned, a community affair and, as its name implied, it was held in the very streets of the town. The little square in the center of the village was blocked off by means of snow fences, so that no automobiles could intrude upon the dance. A bandstand was set up in the middle of the square from which the orchestra would play. Strings of colored lights would outline the dancing area. Members of the community volunteered to serve on refreshment, entertainment and decorating committees. Each year the committees tried to surpass the achievements of the previous year, by varying the decorations or adding novelty dances to the evening's program.

At last the night arrived. Welton, Mavis, Patty and Jo all were going together. The girls began their preparations early, but in spite of this Welton and Mavis were forced to wait for them to finish their primping. Patty and Jo had experimented fixing their hair in different ways, changed their dresses several times, until finally Welton despaired of their ever being ready. He was forced to admit they were worth waiting for when they finally emerged from their bedroom.

Jo was wearing a light green dress whose full skirt just touched the floor. The low neckline was cuffed with a fold of the same material which extended just over the edge of her shoulders and dipped slightly in the back. Her golden tan was effectively set off by the soft green color of the dress. She had parted her hair in the middle and soft curls framed her face. A simple string of pearls circled her throat.

Patty had chosen a white net skirt over a yellow starched cotton underskirt which stood out stiffly about her and rustled as she walked. The top of her dress was also yellow with a square neck. Wide straps of white net were attached in the front and fastened low in the back. Her hair was pulled smoothly across her forehead and caught on one side with a glittering clip. Her eyes shone with anticipation.

Welton stood back and surveyed them like a proud yet wistful parent. Where were the little girls in faded blue jeans who had been there only that morning? They couldn't be the same ones who confronted him now, he thought. These were far too grown-up to be his Patty and Jo.

"You both look gorgeous, darlings," Mavis told them. She, being hardly more than a girl herself, was not quite so shocked at the metamorphosis that had taken place as Welton was.

As they approached the village the twins both gasped at the fairyland which had taken the place of the familiar square. Red and blue and yellow lights twinkled everywhere. Garlands of flowers formed a canopy under which couples were already dancing. The bandstand was decorated to resemble a huge drum. On it sat eight musicians whose music drifted to the dancers in the square and to the watchers beyond. Behind the bandstand at the rear of the square were gaily decorated refreshment booths. On the residential side of the square older people looked out from their porches, nodding and commenting among themselves.

Patty and Jo soon found their friends, who were waiting for them in a laughing group. Dick whirled Jo off down the flower-decked street. Leo shyly asked Patty to dance with him and she found that he danced smoothly and gracefully, although some of the steps he used were new to her.

Some time later Jo and Patty begged their partners to stop and rest. They were surprised to find how hard it was to dance on the hard pavement of the street, which was quite different from a polished dance floor.

"Ooh!" Jo mourned as she limped to a chair with Dick's help. "Why do my feet hurt so? I'm afraid they won't last the night."

"You stay here," Dick ordered, "I'll go and get you some punch. I should have warned you that dancing in the streets is tough. I forget about it from one year's dance to the next, I guess."

"See if you can't find me a tub of hot water instead," Jo called after him. He turned and laughed over his shoulder.

"What's the matter?" asked Patty, coming up to her.

"My feet hurt. Don't yours?" Jo answered. She leaned over and rubbed her instep gingerly.

"I hadn't noticed it, I was having such a good time. Isn't it beautiful here?" She sat down next to Jo and gazed up at the soft lights.

"Lovely," Jo agreed. "Isn't it nice to see everyone joining in this way? Look over there, Pat. There's Elaine's father dancing with little Dorothy Barlett. Only eleven years old, but doesn't she look cute?"

"Oh, and look who's dancing with Mavis. Dr. Gordon, I think it is." Patty scanned the crowd. "Welty's with Dick's mother way over by the bandstand."

Dick returned with two cups of punch and behind him came Leo similarly laden. They handed one to each of the girls and pulled up two chairs beside them.

"Sorry, Jo," Dick said, "the punch bowls are all in use and they didn't have any tubs." He grinned down at her.

"Umm, this is good, anyway," Jo said as she took a long swallow. "I feel better already."

Once refreshed they were ready to dance again. Welton and George Anderson came up to the group and George said, "Here, now, you two can't monopolize these girls all evening. How about giving the rest of us a break? Jo, will you give me the pleasure?"

Welton took Patty by the hand and began to dance to the slow waltz tune that was being played. Leo went off in search of Elaine while Dick found Mavis, still dancing with Dr. Gordon, and cut in on him.

Presently, Leo cut in on Patty again, and, after they had danced a few minutes, he looked down at her and said, "Have I said how lovely you look tonight, Patty? I have thought it from the moment you came."

"It's nice of you to say that, Leo," Patty answered demurely. Then she added, "I wish this evening would never end. It—it's so beautiful."

"I, too," he replied with feeling, "because I must leave tomorrow."

"So soon?" Patty's face fell.

"Yes. I received a letter this morning from the college and they want me to report there in three days. It seems there are more examinations to take and I must register for my room and so on."

"I'll be sorry to see you leave, Leo."

Leo edged her to the side of the crowd and stopped dancing. "There is something you must have before I leave," he said, fishing something from his pocket.

Patty looked and said, "Oh! The little toy drummer. Why, Leo, he's as good as new!"

"You remember that the drum is hollow?"

"Yes, of course. Do you mean that I should open it again?"

"It is nothing, only a little trinket. A joke, perhaps," Leo explained, his eyes showing some amusement.

Patty opened the drum and pulled something soft and silky from the interior. She shook it out and held it in front of her. It was a silk scarf covered with gay little figures that were very similar to the music box figures.

She looked at Leo and laughed. "It's sweet, Leo. And the figures will remind me of you when you are gone."

Leo was serious again as he said, "I hope so.

And we will meet again, perhaps? You mentioned that your college is not far away from mine."

"Of course we will see you often. Welton and Mavis have told you that you are always welcome to come here."

Leo looked down at her and squeezed her hand. "You will regret your standing invitation. I will become a nuisance. Whenever I can get away, I will come and you will hear me knocking on your door."

"That's a chance I'm willing to take," Patty smiled. The music grew loud about them as they stood together.

"Listen," breathed Leo, with a faraway look in his eyes. "They're playing a tarantella. It is a dance we do in Italy." He grabbed her hand and danced off with her, leading her in the fast, intricate steps that he knew so well.

With a flourish the music stopped. Then the band began to play another waltz which signaled the end of the evening. Couples strolled off together and soon the streets were empty. After saying goodnight to Leo and Dick, Jo and Patty went off to find the Duers. Patty told Jo what Leo had told her and showed her the scarf he had given her.

Jo squeezed her sister with delight. "How nice everything has turned out," she said. "Who would have thought that a little toy drummer would be responsible for all that has happened?"

After the night of the street dance, Patty and Jo found themselves busy making preparations for their first taste of college life. There were clothes to buy and packing to be done, so that they had little time for anything else. At last everything was ready and their trunks waited in the hall for Yamoto to take them to the station.

It was their last day at Harker's Cove and nearly all of the summer people had returned to their winter homes. Jo and Patty were having their last swim in the lake with Dick. As they lay in the sand after their swim, they heard Mavis call to them from the cliff.

The urgency in her voice brought them to their feet and they were off at once up the winding path. Dick stayed behind, gathering up their beach robes and towels. At the top of the cliff the girls met Mavis and she told them that Welton wanted to see them.

Wondering why he had sent for them, the girls hurried off to the house with Mavis. They found Welton in his study looking down at a letter in his hand. Evidently it had just come in the afternoon mail.

"Ah," he said, smiling up at the breathless girls, "there you are." He stood up and came around the desk toward them. He put an arm around each of them and held the letter so they could both see it. It began with some very official legal phrases that the twins couldn't understand.

Welton pointed to a sentence and said, "This is the part I want you to read. You see, it says . . ."

Patty and Jo interrupted him, turning their heads to look at his face, "It says you've adopted us! Oh, Welty! Is it true?" They were jumping up and down with delight.

"Yes, my dears, it's true. We've wanted this for some time, but it seemed to take forever." There were tears in his eyes as he smiled down at them.

Mavis came and stood beside him, slipping her hand through his arm. "Our daughters seem to be pleased," she said simply.

Patty and Jo were upon them in a moment, fondly hugging and kissing them. Everyone began laughing and crying at the same time. Lucky began barking, too, sensing excitement in the air. At last the hubbub subsided, but the twins bubbled inside for joy, finding it hard to realize their good fortune.

"Oh, dear," Jo began, "now I don't know if I can bear to leave you. Patty, let's not go to college after all."

"Yes, Jo, let's just stay here with our parents. I can't bear to let them out of my sight."

"We'll still be here," Mavis said, smiling. "My goodness, you wouldn't want to miss the fun of college. You can't imagine what wonderful things are in store for you."

As the train carried Patty and Jo away from home the following day, they wondered how anything could happen that would make them any happier. Their dearest wish had been fulfilled. Was there anything more to come? It was unlikely, they thought, but ahead of them, perhaps, lay new adventures. They could only wait and see.

A Descriptive Catalog of

FALCON BOOKS FOR GIRLS

PATTY AND JO, DETECTIVES—*by Elsie Wright*

THE PROSPECT of a dreary Christmas vacation at Miss Langton's School for Young Ladies is suddenly brightened for the Faraday twins, Patty and Jo, when they receive an invitation from their guardian (whom they have never seen) to visit him. They arrive eagerly at Harker's Cove—only to discover that he has disappeared.

Undaunted by the efforts of the Japanese manservant to keep them from unraveling the mystery, these clever teen-agers become involved in all sorts of adventures. The Faraday twins embody the vivaciousness and self-assurance of all teen-age girls today.

CHAMPION'S CHOICE—*by John R. Tunis*

FROM THE moment Janet Johnson's childish skill with a
tennis racquet attracted the attention of a professional,
tennis became Janet's one love. There were the years of
gruelling practice to perfect the natural aptitude of the
girl, followed by victories at Wimbledon and in the
United States tennis championships. The shy, awkward
girl from the country became a poised, confident young
lady.

Rodney Davis, Janet's childhood friend, played an
important part in Janet's victories with his advice on
tennis strategy, but when he asked Janet to give up her
championship and marry him, she was faced with the
biggest decision in her life. In making her decision, Janet
learned her hardest lesson.

Champion's Choice is filled with the tense and vivid
drama of championship tennis, and the thrilling story of
a "Cinderella" champion.

PENNY ALLEN AND THE MYSTERY OF THE HAUNTED HOUSE—*by Jean McKechnie*

IT ISN'T every day that a family inherits a haunted house. But when Philip Allen, with his brother Jimmy and his sisters Marjorie and Penny, went up to Michigan to investigate their legacy, they discovered they had an uninvited guest. It was the Green Lady, whose ghost was said to haunt Uncle John's lodge. How they solved the mystery and made wonderful new friends is an exciting adventure story all girls will love.

PENNY ALLEN AND THE MYSTERY OF THE HIDDEN TREASURE—*by Jean McKechnie*

WHEN THE Allens—Philip, Jimmy, Penny and Marjorie—opened their Michigan Lodge as a summer hotel, they decided to track down the rumor of buried treasure. Other people, however, had the same idea, and before the Allens could solve the baffling clues they discovered, they found themselves in real danger. How they found the treasure, and how Penny and Philip found romance with it, make an exciting and romantic adventure everyone will enjoy.

JEAN CRAIG GROWS UP—*by Kay Lyttleton*

WHEN Tom Craig came home from the Pacific, wounded, the Craig family found there wasn't enough money to maintain their beautiful home and send Tom to the country to regain his health. So the family moved to a farm in Elmhurst. Lovely Jean, only seventeen, was a staff of courage for her family in their new life. But it wasn't all hard work. There were picnics, new friends, and there was Ralph McRae, the young and handsome landlord.

This is the heart-warming story of a family who met hardship with pluck and humor, and of Jean Craig, gay and lovable, whose courage surmounted all obstacles.

JEAN CRAIG IN NEW YORK—*by Kay Lyttleton*

WHEN LOVELY Jean Craig moved with her family to Woodhow farm in Connecticut, she thought she was giving up her art lessons forever. And then suddenly the opportunity came to go to New York to study, and she went to live with her cousin Beth in the suburbs of New York. These months were an exciting interlude in her life. She loved seeing her old friends again, going to parties, and meeting new people, among them Aldo Thomas, an artist from Italy.

Jean Craig in New York tells of Jean's adventures in the city, but it is also the story of the Craigs who meet life's adventures with gaiety and courage.

JEAN CRAIG FINDS ROMANCE—*by Kay Lyttleton*

JEAN CRAIG had always wanted to be an artist. But when her family had moved to Woodhow in Connecticut, she had given up her art lessons. Later, when she was able to resume them, she realized how important a career was to her. But then Ralph McRae came along, and Jean found herself unable to make up her mind as to what she wanted most. And while Jean was trying to come to a decision, her sister Kit was having a fine adventure of her own out West.

Jean Craig Finds Romance is filled with gaiety and humor, another charming story of the wonderful, courageous Craigs and their family adventures.

JEAN CRAIG, NURSE—*by Kay Lyttleton*

WHEN Jean Craig learned that Elmhurst was planning a hospital, she sponsored a fund-raising barn dance. It proved to be a turning point in her life, for here she met Ted Loring and decided to study nursing. And it was in this profession that she found herself solving problems and even sponsoring a romance in truly exciting fashion. Jean made others happy and found happiness herself in this vivid and absorbing story of hospital life behind the scenes.

JEAN CRAIG, GRADUATE NURSE—*by Kay Lyttleton*

As Jean Craig finished her training and prepared for graduation, illness struck—first in her own family, and later in epidemics that swept the village of Elmhurst. It was with a deep feeling of satisfaction that Jean was able to give trained and efficient aid at the hospital. It was with equal satisfaction that she watched romance blossom between Dr. Benson, the fresh young intern, and Eileen Gordon, the new Supervisor of Nurses, and discovered that her sister Kit was practically engaged. But the joy of the family reached a new peak when Doris, the youngest daughter, won a music scholarship. *Jean Craig, Graduate Nurse* is another heartwarming and happy story about the Craigs of Elmhurst.